TWO SPINSTERS AND A CORPSE

EVE TARRINGTON

Louisa-Margaretta saw the first drop of blood when she was turning to the window, trying to see how deep the snowfall would be.

Except there was no snow, which, given the chill, seemed impossible. She had hoped that at least there would be the small mercy of terrible weather. She might be trapped in a tower, but provided she did not have to entertain strangers, the evening need not be absolutely ruinous.

She saw the second drop of blood when her mother came in the door. She held up her handkerchief.

"It's not a good omen, Mother. Two drops of blood."

Her mother and erstwhile jailer only smiled. "I thought it had to be three to portend death, my dear. You're getting fanciful here in the north."

"You would say that only things in the Bible can be trusted as omens. Forgive me if I have an easier time believing this sort of sign than four silly horsemen who come telling us all that we are doomed."

"I believe because we do not need to stray from the word of God, Louisa-Margaretta. It is all there."

"And those were the teachings you were following when you stole me away and trapped me here at Wycliff Castle, then?"

Something caught her eye for a second time near her window. It was not snow, but perhaps it was a person. Possibly somebody getting in wine or meat, for it was far too cold for anyone to venture out for a walk except her mother, who insisted on the very great effect a bracing walk might have on one's health.

"I did it for your own benefit, my dear," said Mama, more placidly than Louisa-Margaretta would have liked.

"Well, I have benefitted quite enough. Perhaps this little interlude has reached its natural end."

For the first time, Louisa-Margaretta saw that her mother was nettled. In spite of long years of bringing up son after son, followed by a stubborn young daughter who was more trouble than any of the boys, the unshakable Mrs Haddington did have her limits.

"The only natural end," she snapped, "will be a wedding."

Louisa-Margaretta was about to respond to this when she paused. There was one more drop of red in her handkerchief.

There was a reasonable explanation, of course. A young lady who had never had troubles with her nose before might well have some difficulty if she was in a very cold place, frequently weeping, susceptible to illness for the first time in her life.

But she only said, "Three drops. This means a death in the family."

The gown had appeared on Judith's bed just after she refused to go to the ball.

She was wearing a simple black dress which wanted altering, as it had become loose on her small frame. Judith had always been thin, but the past year had worn her down to nothing. Far from suffering over her lost bloom and thin body, she felt like this new appearance suited her spirit. She did not consider herself a saint, but she had begun to understand why ascetics took simple food. Gluttony, which she had always regarded as nothing more than a mild sin, suddenly appeared both pleasurable and dangerous. She had convinced herself that she needed only simple foods, nothing rich, and that she need not bother with balls, teas, or other frivolous things that occupied the hours of certain ladies. After all, her father needed her help with Aaron, Moses, and Joseph, so she needed to stay near her home in any case.

She would never have asked for such a gown, and simply looking on it made her feel just as ill as a hearty serving of rich pudding. Instead of a simple piece in the violet of half-mourning, which she might at least have pretended to consider, the rich scarlet garment had enough lace and ribbons for a whole neighbourhood. Judith hardly recognized the fashions. It had been years since she was last interested in such things and longer still since she had saved enough of her own pin money for a new gown. If it had not been small, perfectly cut for her thin figure, she would have thought it must be for another woman.

But Miriam was the only other young lady in the household, and she had not grown thin. And the fashion would not be suitable for a lady of Aunt Leah's years. In fact, it was also not appropriate for a young girl such as Miriam, who was not out yet and would be expected to wear something much more modest. No, the gown could only be meant for Judith.

That did not mean she had any intention of wearing it.

She knew better than to demand answers from her father, though she did ask him. He was sitting in a chair by the fire while two of her brothers, Aaron and Moses, played on the carpet with wooden animals. Her father must have been one of the only men in England who refused to allow toy soldiers. Instead, he had taken the story of Noah's ark as his inspiration and allowed his children to collect little animals over the years. Judith, at twenty-five, was the eldest, so many of the animals were quite worn, and she was sure at Christmas, a few new ones would make an appearance. In fact, she had meant to find at least one for each of her brothers, but the packing and new arrangements had exhausted her. Surely, someone in Brackenfield, their new village, would be able to make them and might let her have one at a good price. Being a rector's daughter had its privileges, but she knew nobody, and Christmas was approaching.

"Papa," she said. "Why on earth have you bought me a gown?"

She had to repeat this several times. Her father was absorbed in his Bible, and then some mishap with the little wooden horses their Uncle Archibald had whittled for them distracted him. When he slowly rose to his feet, having assured Aaron that even a wobbly horse would have been able to board the ark, he had a look at the red gown that Judith was clutching in her cold fingers.

"I let your aunt choose it, my dear," he said. "She had it made. And one for your sister, of course."

As Judith looked round for her aunt, Miriam came running out with a peach creation pressed to her heart.

"Oh, it is lovely!" she said. "Judith, only look. I don't care how rich the Haddington family is or how beautiful Miss Haddington is reputed to be, we will outshine any of them tonight!"

"Miriam," warned their father, but he could not help smiling at the sight. Miriam was radiant, her face alight at the idea of the first ball she would ever attend. Though Judith and Miriam both had their mother's wide eyes and fair skin, they looked as if they were separated by more than six years. Judith was thin and pale, her straight hair arranged in a style that was severe and practical. She had insisted on shaving her head after their mother died because she had read it was a practice observed by certain men in the Orient. It seemed to be the only thing befitting the way she felt — cold and bereft. Now that it had been over a year, her hair was long enough that she could get it out of the way, but it could not be put in pretty braids and curls like her sister's. When she had to go out, she wore a wig, but at home, she found it too much of a bother.

Miriam was pretty and plump, and were it not for the circumstances of their mourning, Judith was sure she would have been an acknowledged beauty. Her dark hair glistened in the light, and her high spirits made her lovelier still. Her bright-blue eyes were shining with excitement. Indeed, she nearly had been considered a beauty years ago, but a girl with no fortune who was not yet out could hardly expect to attract open admiration.

"I am sure you will enjoy the ball," said Judith. "I do not plan to go and could never wear such a dress."

"Only think," pleaded Miriam. She did not attempt to speak to her father but stood facing her sister, still holding the peach-coloured gown. "I was ready to be out two years ago, Mama and Papa had agreed, and I am quite ready now. It is my first ball, and if you are so selfish as to stay home, Papa will not let me attend. You know that he always wishes us to be a pair when we are with strangers."

"It's only the Haddingtons," Judith said. "If they could find more families of their set willing to join them in Derbyshire, they would not have invited us. And it's not as if you need a chaperone. Aunt Leah will be with you, as well as Papa."

"Fine," said Miriam, keeping a bit of sweetness in her face until their father turned to fetch his sister. As soon as he was out of the room, she glared at Judith.

"There is no need to think only of yourself," she said. "Aunt Leah went to a great deal of trouble to have these made for us, and I know yours was the more expensive."

Judith could only sigh. "I didn't wish for any gown, Miriam. She could have asked me."

"What good would that have been, when I knew you would refuse?" said a tall, handsome woman, sweeping into the room before her diminutive brother as if she were the sole owner of the rectory.

"Aunt Leah," cried Aaron and Moses, rising from the floor to embrace their aunt and tell her all about their adventures with the animals.

Before Judith could confront her, Aunt Leah had swept Moses outside, claiming that the child would faint without a bit of fresh air. She was fond of saying that a good walk could cure any ill. Judith, in her grief, had begun to find this saying intolerable.

Moses, at seven years old, hated being confined to the fireside more than anyone else in the family. Though they were not used to the chilly wind, he was eager to use his skipping rope, even if his hands froze. And he wanted his aunt to learn all about it too. The sound of their laughter came through the windows, though they were firmly shut against the cold.

"Papa," said Miriam. "Tell Judith there is nothing wrong in it, please."

"I am sure there is not, my dear," said their father gravely. "Do you think it improper?"

Judith looked at her dress again, inspired.

"I will, that women adorn themselves in modest apparel," she said, the quotation rolling off her tongue easily. She tried to compose her cross expression into one of angelic piety. *Fordyce's Sermons*, though dull and silly, did have their uses.

Her father frowned. "Do you find the gown immodest, then? I thought, since it was chosen by your aunt, that it would be fitting for such an occasion."

"You have no opinion of your own, father?" teased Judith, but her father was immune to her teasing. Miriam, however, had never taken kindly to her older sister's jokes. And now she was prepared for a battle.

"Never spend too much time or thought on the embellishment of the body, but always prefer the graces of the mind," she said sweetly. "St Paul was quite wise, of course."

Judith frowned. "St Paul?"

Their father smiled. "Yes, my dear. Miriam, you have been reading, I see! Very good."

He made to leave, and Judith put a hand on his arm. "Father, as Miriam just reminded us, St Paul told us not to spend our time on embellishments such as dresses."

He did not have a moment to respond before Miriam cut in.

"But you are spending a great deal of time on it, dearest sister, by arguing against it. Why not just wear it and go, and think of your mind instead?"

There were more sounds of laughter from the frozen ground. Joseph must have convinced Aaron to leave the fireside and take him out to look at the skipping rope, though at only three years old, he did little more than toss the thing about and call it a "snake snake" as he laughed. Aunt Leah may not have had any children, but in entertaining her nieces and nephews, she was often more spirited than a natural parent. It was one reason that Judith had always got on quite well with her aunt before the present visit.

The love between the two had unravelled when Aunt Leah started trying to interest Judith in frivolous things like balls and gentleman callers. She had hoped that her aunt might be understanding, as Miss Leah St Clair was herself unmarried, but apparently, Judith's mother had set her sister-in-law the task of marrying off both Miriam and Judith.

To Judith, it was a form of torture and the only thing that made her admit that her mother had not been of sound mind in her final weeks on earth.

Their father managed to leave the room. He must have known the battle was not over, but he had expressed one thought and would now leave his two daughters to express ever so many more. Judith threw the gown on a nearby chair and faced her sister. "St Paul? You could not possibly have remembered any of his writings. You always claimed that they put you to sleep."

Miriam gave a wicked grin. "You ought never to ask a lady the source of her information. And I am sure I should not reveal it in any case."

There was a sound of pain from the outside, but Judith

refused to go to her brothers before she got an answer. "Tell me."

Judith was always more serious than Miriam but rarely angry. Something in her tone unsettled her sister.

Miriam frowned. "Very well. I heard you giving Papa trouble, and I grabbed his copy of *Fordyce's Sermons* before I came in."

Judith stared at her sister, which only seemed to amuse Miriam. If she had been cowed by Judith's anger, in recounting her little triumph, she blossomed once again.

"It was in the first chapter!" she said, gleeful. "And what's more, old Fordyce was arguing against St Paul's words. *He* seemed to think that it was not so terrible for a young lady to have a bit of a care as regards her appearance. You see, dear Judith, if even old Fordyce is not on your side, you have no chance with Papa."

Judith grabbed for the gown, and Miriam only just whisked it away in time.

"You can't force me to go," Judith said, "and neither can Papa. What, would you drag me into the carriage? Say what you like, but I shall not attend."

They heard their aunt calling them. Both saw her through the window, huddled on the ground as her three nephews looked on, ready to cry. In fact, Moses had already started crying. He was the quickest to run out and to make any game rougher, but he often ended up in tears.

Miriam froze, and Judith ran outside, sinking to her knees beside her aunt. She took Moses into her lap and motioned to Aaron that he ought to take Joseph back into the house. Judith was used to being the eldest, the sibling expected to have a care when something went awry. Arguing against things did not come easily to her, but soothing bruises certainly did.

"Tell me, Aunt Leah," she said. "Shall we send for the

doctor?" With Judith's aid, the dignified lady hobbled to her feet, and they made for the door and the warmth of the house.

"I am quite well, my dear," she said. "But I cannot possibly walk on this knee. So you will need to accompany your sister."

❊   3   ❊

As their carriage approached Wycliff Castle, Judith began to shiver. The large stone house, though it was very grand, did not seem to have either the ornamentation or the enchanted nature that would have befitted a real castle. Instead, its looming figure and many windows made Judith think only of money, and she wondered what on earth she was supposed to say to people who had such a very great deal of it. She wished that it would snow. It was a persistent argument between the sisters — whether snow made winter warmer and more bearable or whether it was only a tedious addition to an already intolerable season. On this evening, it seemed that it would have made little difference. The wind was bitter, and Judith looked in vain for the last light of the sun. Though she knew in her heart that Derbyshire was not quite far enough from their former home for the days to be appreciably shorter, still, it felt that she had come to a place where the winter in the high peaks would be particularly unforgiving.

And she knew the journey back to Essex, or even simply to London, would be a long one. Even by stagecoach, with the money that her father was earning in his lucrative new living, the travel would be arduous and costly. So she may as well have been in the wilds of Scotland or even in Iceland, trapped for the winter. Though she longed to travel and see her friends, unless she found a way to become very wealthy, that would not be anywhere in her future.

Judith longed for the Christmas gatherings that used to characterize the season. The old vicarage was small, so of necessity, parties were both loud and cosy. The children and the adults were all together, and though there was no room for dancing, everyone played music and sang ever more loudly as they drank elder wine. Indeed, Judith had some proficiency on the pianoforte and was happy to play carols while others warbled along. She amused herself by rewriting the tunes, often to her father's disapprobation and her mother's amusement. Her jaunty rendition of an operatic aria, with the words of "God Rest Ye Merry Gentlemen," had been so offensive to her father that she had resolved only to play it when he was safely out of the house. To her father, the hymns were sacred, but to Judith, the tunes were lovely little puzzles.

The church she grew up in, the Church of St Helen and St Giles, was built in Norman times, so old that generations of the living and the dead had thought it part of the very bones of the countryside. Because the church had such a long life, what had once been the rectory had been passed from rich family to rich family. The St Clair family had to live in a little vicarage that was not quite as near as they might have hoped, but Judith never minded. She thought there was something holy about an old building with worn stones and solid construction. It was better than the church her father had taken over, which was of a very different style, one designed to impress rather than endure.

Now they were to pass their first Christmas in Derbyshire. It was also to be their first Christmas of festive traditions without their mother. The Christmas before, the family had all been in mourning, and the celebration had been limited to what was required of her father. There were no callers, and as long as they went to services, they were able to banish the whole season without much thought. Though her father did not stop speaking of it entirely, he spent large parts of each day with his books. Miriam stayed by their aunt's side, Judith took to her bed, and their younger brothers spent nearly all of their days playing with neighbours.

This year, Judith had prepared herself for a Christmas that was strange and lonely. Now, apparently, she was to celebrate Christmas in the style of a grand lady. She would not have wished for a repetition of the year before, but neither did she enjoy the prospect of what her father generally deemed "sad frivolity" and what she considered a trial of a party.

When she stepped into the house, however, she forgot her cares for a moment. Though the greenery that would characterize the later parts of the season had not yet been put up, the house they had entered was festive and bright. No expense had been spared on candles, clearly, and the flash of gowns and jewels in the bright lights made Judith feel transported. She could not even try to frown when she heard strains of music. The tune was familiar to her, as she had played it many times, but the ensemble was not. How different the notes were when played by a group of instruments together! Her sad little rendition on the pianoforte could not compare. The grand entrance of the large home was gleaming, and its furnishings appeared to be expensive and fashionable. Since Judith had not met the neighbours, she recognized no one, though Miriam prodded her sister every so often to point out the few neighbours that she had met during calls with their father. Miriam had avoided most of the calls themselves, as they bored her, but now, she was ready to pester her father for introductions.

Judith struggled to collect her thoughts as Papa drew them over to their host and hostess. The host looked red-cheeked and uncomfortable, a short man who was strong and solid without being fat. Like Judith, his hair was dark and mousy, his nose thin and unbecoming. She felt sorry for her host, as she saw many of the things she had always disliked about her own appearance reflected in his. To add to this, he could hardly put two words together. Judith wondered whether he was very stupid indeed or merely shy. She considered herself shy, but even she did better than this man when called upon to show politeness.

Of course, he had little need to speak, as there was a very able woman who spoke for him. It was clear that he was one of the many plain men who had managed to marry an exceedingly beautiful wife. The hostess, Mrs Haddington, was dressed simply but with great elegance in a deep-green gown. Even if Judith had not previously learnt from Miriam that Mr Haddington was a tradesman of humble origins, and his wife was an accomplished woman from a large, aristocratic family, their appearance and manners would have brought her to that conclusion at once.

"Your lovely daughters," Mrs Haddington cooed to Judith's father, beaming at the family. "You must be Miss St Clair and Miss Miriam St Clair? Delighted. I cannot tell you how blessed we are to have such a gifted rector in our neighbourhood, and we are thrilled to welcome you as part of the family."

Judith bristled. In her eyes, the candles dimmed, and she saw the ball once more for what it was. She was not in fairyland, she was at the home of her father's patroness, a woman who was well meaning but clearly insensible. Judith was certainly not part of this stranger's family, though she was not silly enough to offend the person who held the livelihood of the St Clair family in her power. However much Judith hated the lacy red gown that she was wearing, she was quite sensible of cost. It was the only garment she owned that made her look elegant rather than ill, and she was sure that was due to the skill of the dressmaker and the quality of the material. It would not do to insult the woman who had allowed them to afford both.

"Delighted to make your acquaintance," she murmured, while Miriam only blushed.

"My dear, sweet girls," said Mrs Haddington, unwilling to let her guests go. "I do hope you will soon meet my daughter, Louisa-Margaretta. You are all new to the neighbourhood, are you not? But at least the two of you have each other. My darling needs a friend or a sister," she said, pressing Judith's hand between both of hers, and Mr Haddington started at this.

"Young ladies like company," he said in a rough voice that sounded a bit louder than the whisper of moments before. "And that's all, my dear."

Mrs Haddington nodded. "Quite. I tell you, I will be delighted to introduce you all, if only I can find out where she has gone! The house is new, you see, so we are constantly searching for each other."

For the first time, there was worry behind her wide smile, but Miriam nodded. "I am sure we shall see her before too long."

Mrs Haddington nodded. "You are too good, dear. The truth is, we have three gentlemen staying, so it is lovely that you have come, and I must find my daughter! I should hate to see any of my dear nephews sitting idle for want of a partner."

Miriam looked rather too eager to be introduced to the "dear" nephews, and Judith succeeded in steering her away.

Once they were a safe distance from Mr and Mrs

Haddington, she sighed. "Papa, we have come and paid our respects. And now, I only wish that we could leave. I should be happy to plead a sick headache. And should we not use caution, given the season? I am afraid we will encounter difficulties getting home. The weather is sure to turn."

"We do not live far away, my dear," he said. "I am sure no horse would be unable to find her way to the edge of the property in a storm. And I see this as an opportunity to meet my flock. Perhaps you can assist me. Mr and Mrs Chant are over there. The whole family paints, I believe, except the mother. Three daughters, though they are rather younger than you are. I know that there, in the corner, is a Mrs Maxwell, a widow who lives in the village with her sister."

Though Judith had not met Mrs Maxwell, she had heard her father mention the woman's name, and she looked at her hosts with some curiosity. In London, a woman of Mrs Maxwell's standing would never have been invited to a ball in such a grand home. In their little village back in Essex, a woman such as Mrs Maxwell might receive visits of charity from a grand lady, but she would not be found taking refreshments in a castle with all of the grandest local families. Judith concluded that there must be something in the country manners of Derbyshire that she did not yet understand. Failing that, their hosts must have very curious ideas about the villagers.

In spite of this very interesting detail, Judith still did not wish to pass the evening with Mrs Maxwell or other ladies of advanced years. The idea of slipping away to gossip with Miriam suddenly seemed a little less odious. Accompanying her father about, ready to lecture on the subject of remembering that balls and puddings were secondary to the spiritual meaning of Christmas, was a task that Judith always tried to avoid.

"Perhaps I ought to go with Miriam," she said. "I am her

chaperone, after all. I would very much like the chance to admire this beautiful home before we all must sit and eat."

Her father, knowing that she was uninterested in architecture, frowned. "Are you sure, my dear?"

"Yes," she said, but it was too late to escape over to the wall where Miriam stood, smiling a bit too brightly as she fingered the ribbons on her gown.

There was a gentleman approaching them.

"A pleasure to see you again," said her father placidly, turning to his daughters.

He beckoned to Miriam so that he would have both of his daughters near him, and she came at once, no doubt drawn to the presence of one of the gentlemen of the family.

"My dears, let me present Mr Morgan Ramsbury."

They were introduced to the man who had walked over, a bit too quickly, to speak with them. Judith wondered if he had been sent by his aunt to ask one of the two sad, friendless Miss St Clairs to dance. Indeed, though he had approached them at a brisk pace, after the introduction itself, he had little to say.

Judith realized that her father had met Mr Morgan Ramsbury once, but he had not provided them with much of an account of the man. After meeting him, this made sense to her.

Mr Morgan Ramsbury, it appeared, was not a man of much conversation. His countenance might have been called handsome, except it was just as constrained as Mr Haddington's.

"How do you find Derbyshire?" he said, barely looking at her, after her father had been called away to another parishioner.

"It is rather chilly," said Judith, and he smiled.

"Quite."

There was a pause so long she wondered whether her

father might break it on his eventual return. It seemed unlikely that Mr Morgan Ramsbury would say anything that was not a response to a direct question. Miriam ended up being the one to continue the conversation.

"Do you often spend Christmas here?" she asked, her smile warm and open.

"We are here at my aunt's invitation and Mr Haddington's," he said. "As the family has only been settled here for a month, it is my first Christmas in Derbyshire."

"And ours," said Miriam.

"Indeed," he murmured. Then he blinked. "I see the dancing is to continue."

"Yes," said Judith. "But we are a rector's daughters, both of us, and thus neither accomplished dancers nor eager ones."

"Quite," he said again, and bowed to both of them. "Well. I wish you ladies an enjoyable evening."

4

As he left, Judith stared after him. There was something about Mr Morgan Ramsbury that she found quite unsettling. Perhaps it was the way he didn't wish to meet her eye or his lack of conversation.

"You needn't refuse for the both of us," snapped Miriam. "There was no need to be so rude."

"There is no need for you to be rude to me, either, and yet, here we stand," said Judith, beginning to glare at the musicians. She suddenly felt angry at the whole Ramsbury family and the Haddingtons with them. It was unpardonable that anyone should have money to buy such a monstrous, large building and have the conceit to live there. And to offer her father so much money that he found it imperative to uproot his whole family. It was as if their income were a large club, too unwieldy to hold, heavy enough to damage everything in sight.

Miriam gave a sigh then began an impression of a young lady being properly presented in London. "This is a lovely occasion for my coming out, dear sister. I feel just as if I am being presented at court. Oh, look! I do not know how I missed the queen. There she is, just there."

Judith did not think the joke was particularly amusing, especially as she herself was very much inclined to wish that their country were ruled by a queen rather than a profligate regent. Still, she was reminded of her own coming out. Her mother, in spite of her nerves and watchful eyes, had been excited to share the world of adulthood with her daughter. And she was quite clear with Judith that she did not see marriage as a requirement. She had always been firm upon that point, at least until her mysterious deathbed instructions to Aunt Leah. In the years before she died, Mama had been positively sanguine about the many blessings that spinsterhood might hold for either or both of her daughters, though even then, it had hardly seemed likely that Miriam would choose to forgo marriage if she had any real prospects.

"I think spinsterhood sounds rather delightful. But don't share my views on matrimony with your father, dear," she told Judith more than once, her voice lowered playfully, her eyes twinkling. "They would only upset him."

She was, of course, not a stupid woman, and she was always sure to share the perils of spinsterhood with her daughters as well.

"Any child a married woman bears is her husband's," she told them. "But if you do not wish to marry, you mustn't let your heart run away with you."

Judith always responded to this with blushes and vexation. Let her heart run away with her! She was not particularly prone to strong feelings. To her, parties used to be enjoyable, but none of the gentlemen ever seemed in danger of winning her heart.

Of course, they were not the sort of the family whose daughters were presented at court. The gatherings they did attend were much more humble. Still, at her first ball, Judith had felt every bit as eager to dance every dance, to be seen as a young woman, as any of the ladies who curtsied to the queen must have felt.

And for the first season, and the second, and even the third, she had continued to enjoy herself. Though the parties were simple and some of the gossip was tedious, she had never tired of the music. She had even thought that she felt the beginnings of affection once or twice, if not love. But somehow, when her mother became ill, she had ceased to think about any of it. And tonight, her period of wearing full mourning in public had ended, and she seemed to be quite decidedly a spinster. Even Mr Morgan Ramsbury had hardly deigned to speak to her, though he seemed interested enough in beautiful Miriam.

Perhaps it was time to accept her new station. If she could not be a charming young lady, she could at least become an adequate chaperone.

"I will be kinder to the next one, for your sake," she said. "Look! Father has found another gentleman. I promise to go over and beg him to dance with you. Only, I will be sure to imitate the way you used to look at Wynn when you wanted a bit of pastry. I will not give the appearance of begging."

This got a smile out of Miriam. She was, Judith realized belatedly, close to tears. Judith straightened her shoulders. She had been failing to take her mother's place or even her aunt's. She dragged her sister over to where her father stood with the gentleman, determined to be much more than civil.

The introductions were made, and it turned out that this was the brother of the man Judith had just waved off. But this was young Mr Theo Ramsbury, his father's heir, and both his manners and his looks were remarkable. He was not nearly as tall as his brother, and his complexion was darker, but he shared the same brilliant-blue eyes.

"It is a pleasure to meet you, Miss St Clair, Miss Miriam

St Clair," he said, managing to bestow the same brilliant smile on both sisters at once. "I have heard much about you."

"Really, sir? From what source?" said Judith, forgetting again that she was supposed to be kind to this man for Miriam's sake. She felt rather than saw Miriam bristle beside her. Miriam had immediately stood straighter when Mr Theo Ramsbury was introduced to them, and Judith could tell that her sister already felt partial to the impressive young man.

Fortune was kind to her, and Mr Ramsbury was not offended. "From your father, of course! He is quite proud of all his children, as he should be," he said, turning his smile toward Judith's father. All three of them were now smiling, and Judith saw that Mr Ramsbury was one of the happy people who could bring gladness and amusement to an entire family with only the simplest of compliments.

"You are too kind, sir," she said, but she began to mean it. She had forgotten that her father needed the comfort and company offered by a ball, perhaps more than either of his daughters.

"Nonsense! Miss St Clair, may I take this opportunity of asking you for the next two dances?"

"Certainly," she replied, still smiling.

It was only when the dance itself began that she saw Miriam's expression. Instead of helping her sister, Judith had taken another false step. Because she was now dancing with the handsomest gentleman in the room while her sister stood at the edge of the crowd, scowling.

But she had little time to think of it, because Mr Theo Ramsbury was apparently determined to be an attentive partner while dancing.

"How shall you spend Advent, then, Miss St Clair?" he asked. "I hope your father's profession does not mean you have to spend hours arranging boughs in a frozen chapel."

Judith was silent for a moment. In fact, seeing to the church decorations had always been an activity that she enjoyed, but she knew that religion was not fashionable amongst the rich when it involved anything beyond weekly attendance. And she recalled that she was more likely to be engaged in fixing church doors than she was in decorating. Her father said that someone had been trying to get into the chapel, perhaps to sleep, as the nights were very cold.

Judith had promised to check the doors with him and to help him find a locksmith in the village. Her papa was hesitant, because he wanted to offer a warm place to any soul without a home, but he thought it was best not to have anyone sleeping in the church.

"We can fix up one of the cottages at the back of the gardens," he said. "They are small, but they will be warmer."

Judith, clearing her throat, remembered that she was supposed to be talking about the amusements of Advent. The trouble was, she could not think of what they might be in the frozen wilds of Derbyshire.

"I suppose I shall see more of our new home," she said. The word "home" felt like a betrayal on her tongue, and she gave a silent apology to their dear old village of Greenhill for using the sacred word to describe what felt like a place of exile, not belonging. "Though I am not sure how. Even the shortest path can be quite dangerous if it is icy."

"A horse would be safe," he said. "They know very little and yet never seem to lose their footing in winter. Tell me, do you plan to make use of our stables? I believe most of the beasts from my uncle's old country house remain there, but I know of several who have managed the journey. In fact, many of them have done much better than the furniture."

Judith wondered why her Aunt Leah expected her to find a husband at such a gathering. This Mr Theo Ramsbury, with his fine clothes and talk of horses, would hardly consider the degradation of a match with either her or Miriam. Even the second son, Mr Morgan Ramsbury, had been so rich that she had felt perfectly safe in ignoring him. She tried not to sigh.

"I am not a great rider," she said. "We never had more than one horse, so I learned, but I am certainly no expert. I should not know what to do in a hunt."

"My cousin Louisa-Margaretta is a spectacular huntress," he said. "A fine horsewoman. I could not be more different from her."

"Indeed," said Judith, frowning a bit at the mention of Miss Haddington. Miriam had seen the young lady of the house from a distance and was completely in awe of her riding habit, her seat, and her horse, not to mention her beautiful golden hair.

Judith noticed, not for the first time, that the famed Miss Haddington had still not put in an appearance. Even for her sort, this was shockingly rude. Perhaps the rumours about the young lady being too wild for her parents to control were true.

"Perhaps she could teach you," Judith said. It was the mildest comment she could think of.

Mr Ramsbury was laughing.

"Thank goodness she has not forced me to learn," he said. "I should much rather be in town this time of year, or anywhere but this county of ice, snow, and very large rocks. These country sports bore me."

"You do not take after your cousin, then?" she asked, and he shook his head as emphatically as he could while keeping time in the dance.

"We are all to go fox hunting," he said. "Though, I confess, I shall be hunting for the horse least likely to throw me. Imagine!"

Though she did not wish to betray any enjoyment to her

sister, she found herself laughing. It was as if the setting had conspired to change her. A beautiful gown, a handsome gentleman, and the knowledge that Christmas approached were all having the intended effect on her spirits, no matter how much she railed against the Haddingtons and their palatial home.

5

Judith had been given a wise piece of advice about balls many years ago from one of her oldest friends. Of course, Letty Radcliffe was lost to her now. They were doomed to communicate only using letters, and even for the most momentous of occasions, they would not be able to meet.

Even before they were spinsters, Lucia had given her advice about balls. Well, Lucia was not quite a spinster. There was something about her air, her openness, that marked her as a young woman with great wit and little money. That meant she might have difficulty finding a husband, not that she had no prospects at all. For Judith, things were quite different. She felt as if she had been a spinster all her life. She certainly was one now.

Lucia had said that balls were uniformly dull, and there was only one way to cope with them. "Find a friend," she said. "And go for a walk."

At the time, Judith had protested that she had few friends at such assemblies. Her mother and father were determined that she should be admitted to gatherings of people who likely considered themselves her social superiors. They told Judith that she was their equal but never quite understood that she preferred simpler gatherings where she would not be lonely.

"Then find a young woman of quality," said Lucia. "Preferably someone who finds the whole thing as dull as you do. And go off with her. Only make sure you don't get separated, and that your chaperones don't give you away once you are back."

At the happiest of balls, this was a perfect description of Lucia and Judith themselves. Though Judith's mother never approved of Judith's shameless attempts to miss most of the dancing, she was happy if her daughter was with Lucia and always had some polite excuse about the young ladies' whereabouts. After all, as strict as some of the mamas were, their sharp eyes generally did not extend to the powder room. Respectable young ladies, as a pair, could have some degree of freedom that they would not have had alone.

This time, Judith was quite alone. She was a chaperone, of course, so she was supposed to stay with Miriam, but there would be nothing disreputable about her leaving the dancing. And Miriam was so furious that there was little point in staying.

Judith had come over to stand with Miriam after she finished dancing with Mr Ramsbury, only to discover that nobody had asked Miriam to dance. The poor thing was flushed and humiliated.

"Mr Ephraim Ramsbury came over to speak with Papa," she murmured. "We were introduced, and he did not even speak of dancing! He is a physician, and he would go on about all sorts of diseases and cures and every dull thing. He even said that he was christened here, in this very village, because he was born here when his parents were passing through on a journey somewhere else. As if I care about his christening! Too many gentlemen here, and still none of them will dance with me." She was trying to be brave, but her lip trembled in just the way Moses's had when he was crying for Aunt Leah earlier in the day.

Judith looked about, but the next dance had started, and it did seem as if there were more gentlemen than ladies. Overall, there were not many young people dancing. Most of the visitors appeared to be either married or children, and she imagined that many of the families living in Derbyshire already knew each other and might not be eager to give the wrong impression to a vicar's daughter.

A rector's daughter, she reminded herself. Her father was no longer a vicar. But the difference in pay was as nothing to families like the Haddingtons. If they were to be at all mercenary in their marriages, they would be looking for brides with a fortune of at least five thousand pounds, very likely more.

"Miriam," she said, "we only have to stay here, and eventually, one of the gentlemen will wish to dance. Or I can go and be introduced to this Mr Ephraim Ramsbury, then ask if he might help even the numbers. I see Mr Fletcher is not dancing, but I wonder if he dances at all. His brother, Mr Colin Fletcher, seems the likelier dancer, but I have not seen him."

Judith hoped that she had remembered their names. She had pleaded a sick headache when the Fletcher family came to call. She had to piece together what she had seen from her bedroom window with her general impression of the young men.

She realized that she was rambling a bit. In fact, she was rather glad that Mr Colin Fletcher had not come, as he was a charming young gentleman, and Miriam would have been most put out if she had not got to dance with him. With the Mr Ramsburys, at least, she seemed to have more interest in appearances than in the men themselves.

Judith cleared her throat, trying to keep her voice low.

"Mr Ephraim Ramsbury, as a member of the family, is perhaps our most logical choice."

"He is ancient," sniffed Miriam. "You will only ask him to dance with you, anyway. Perhaps you would be well suited."

Judith sighed. She could stand in a ballroom and listen to her sister calling her ancient, which would quickly turn into calling her ugly. Judith's nose and face were thinner than all her siblings, her eyes were muddier, her hair was flat and unimpressive. Where Aaron had eyes as bright as the sky on a spring morning, Judith had eyes the color of mud. Moses had eyelashes that any lady would envy, thick and long, but Judith's lashes were thin. And Miriam, well, she was simply a beauty in every sense. Miriam had not mentioned Judith's notable lack of physical splendor during their period of mourning, but now that she had gone from wistful to furious, she might well decide to go on about all of them.

Vanity had never been one of Judith's vices, at least not when she was happy. But now, trapped in a fine but frozen home, without her mother or any of her friends, she felt that her looks were a curse. They were especially galling when all of her siblings happened to have been blessed with great beauty.

"Papa," said Judith when the two of them caught up to her father. He was in what she and Lucia had always called the "invalid nook" with the elderly widows, holding forth on one of his favourite subjects, a modern-day Bethlehem. Or rather, what a modern-day Bethlehem would be like if the Christ child were to be born in England.

"No crib for a bed," he was saying. "And yet kings were

visiting, in the form of the wise men! Only think of it. If royalty were to visit a family who were staying in these very stables for want of a room at one of our inns, it would make quite a story. Yes, indeed, it would."

"Papa," said Judith again. "I must step away for a bit, but I know Miriam was hoping to sit with you."

Her father performed the introductions, and Judith faithfully repeated and forgot every single name before she fled.

She could not run away from the ballroom as she wished, because a family party had rudely clustered around one door. A woman who was not as old as the ladies sitting with her father but well past her first youth was holding court. She spoke with a curious accent that did not quite fit anywhere in England yet was not as faithful to her native Scotland as it might have been. She was standing rather close to a gentleman in an extraordinary purple tailcoat, whose pale skin and curly hair marked him as another person who did not seem to have Ramsbury or Haddington blood. There was a certain resemblance that most of them shared, but the loquacious Scottish lady and the taciturn gentleman looked quite different.

Judith knew that the lady was Scottish because she was boasting about her life in Gretna Green.

"Famous, isn't it, and the stories are all true. All kinds of couples coming up, long journeys, to wed over the anvil. And a marriage, isn't it, records and everything, no matter whether they announce it or not."

Mrs Haddington, the hostess, touched her husband's arm and smiled. "Well, I'm sure you have many stories, dear Matilda. I must tend to our guests."

Mr Haddington did not look too pleased as she waltzed off, but one of the older gentlemen there looked even more displeased. "I don't know that the young people wish to hear all about Gretna Green," he said. "After all, they should be dancing." That gentleman was not as stout as Mr Haddington, and he looked more tired. He seemed quite ready to escape the ball out of indisposition rather than lack of inclination for such a social gathering. Mr Haddington, though he was clearly none too pleased to be entertaining a great deal of family and strangers, had a natural strength and vitality that was not lost even in the richly lit room and cheerful music.

"Indeed, Papa," said Mr Theo Ramsbury, Judith's dance partner of a few minutes before. "There are not a great many young ladies here, and if I am not introduced to them all, I might be forced to sit out much of the night. Imagine!"

Judith looked over at Miriam. If only she knew that Mr Theo Ramsbury was seeking partners! That was probably why he had asked her to dance. It was senseless to pretend otherwise. At the time, she had hoped it was because her red gown was becoming, but perhaps it was not.

The elderly gentleman grabbed the eager young man's arm. "A word with you first, Theo, if you please," he said.

"Morgan, Ephraim, go and dance," said the Scottish woman to the other young Ramsbury men, both of whom had been silent. "I'm sure you have also had quite enough of my stories." Her eyes settled on Judith rather too quickly, and before she could suggest a partner, Judith nodded quietly and forced her way through the party as politely as she could. She did not wish to dance with Mr Morgan Ramsbury, who had barely spoken to her. She certainly did not wish to face the humiliation of being the "old" partner for Mr Ephraim Ramsbury, the other unmarried gentleman.

As she passed him, it occurred to her that he was neither terribly old nor completely lacking in looks himself, in spite of Miriam's condemnation. True, his hair was turning grey, but his face would have been handsome if not for its sour expression.

"Excuse me," she said. "Pardon me."

As she left, she heard the other older gentleman saying to Mr Haddington, "Stories of old times, eh? Puts me in mind of my own boyhood, so it does, and summers in the country."

Mr Haddington turned to a latecomer and gruffly introduced the old man as a Mr Horace Ramsbury, father of Mr Morgan and Mr Theo Ramsbury. If he hoped that this would put an end to the older man's reminiscences, he was much mistaken. The indefatigable Mr Horace Ramsbury went on about summers in the country and his glorious youth. He made it all sound so idyllic that Judith frowned. Though her childhood had certainly had its beauty, she never would have described it so romantically. Perhaps she would feel differently when she was much older.

Outside the ballroom, the house was quiet and cool. Though Judith had almost been on the point of fanning herself after the dancing, as soon as she was away from the crowd, the heat ceased to disturb her. However, she did see servants and guests moving about, so she knew that she needed to find a place where she could be settled if she were not to have her integrity compromised. Moving freely through a grand home, claiming that she was looking for a retiring room, was all very well for a spinster. But if she were to encounter a gentleman and they were to have a conversation, she might find herself in difficulties quickly. No matter how innocent the conversation, it would not be at all proper.

Finding herself in a hallway with ceilings that seemed almost obscenely high, she thought about where a library might be situated. It would be just her luck to walk straight into a breakfast room or a room that was private for the family. A library was also supposed to be private, but the thought of a book was enough to tempt her.

Judith did not cry easily, but the memory of choosing books to leave behind before their move north was enough to make her teary. She had wept and wept at the time and cursed the Haddingtons and their patronage.

A servant girl passed by, her eyes averted. A housemaid, perhaps? Judith managed to stop her.

"I'm so sorry, I was looking for the library?"

She did not give a reason. She only succeeded in lying when she told a partial truth, never when she invented a history.

"Of course," said the young girl. "It's just up those stairs, second on the left."

There were a great many stairs, and by the time Judith made it to the top of them, she had to catch her breath and had forgotten half of the instructions. On the third try, she found the library. It was ostentatious and grand, but the books were beautiful. She found herself quite in awe of the collection. Since the family was new, she wondered if they had brought the books with them or purchased the collection from their predecessors. She had even heard of some very grand families hiring scholars to not only purchase books but also supervise their arrangement on special shelves. In fact, many of those families were probably just like the Haddingtons, making money hand over fist from industry in Manchester. The very idea of this practice had always amused Judith. The rich, it appeared, would pay for anything.

She took several turns around the room, walking with much more grace, elegance, and true amusement than she had been able to summon in either of the dances. Deciding that she should settle on a book, as she surely could not steal away for the entire ball, she took out a volume of Shakespeare. Though her father tended to disapprove of the plays themselves, he did acknowledge certain similarities between the poetic language of their translations of the Bible and the Bard's work. And she must read something familiar — she could not bear to pick a new novel then leave it half finished when she rushed off to supper. And she would, of course, hurry back to the ball. Quite soon. She fully intended to return, she told herself as she settled into one of the more comfortable chairs.

"What on earth are you about?"

She was out of the seat before she had a moment to think, the beautifully bound volume of *The Tempest* falling to the floor.

When their parents were cross, Miriam immediately told a lie or tried to correct her sister if Judith had the temerity to go first. Judith herself was incapable of thinking on her feet in that manner. "I was hoping to read," she said with as much dignity as she could manage.

"Well, I'm sure that as a guest, your place is not in the library," said the person who stood before her.

She was a woman, at least Judith's age, of wealth and beauty. Her gown, in sharp contrast to Judith's red, was of a pale blue and would have almost looked like the violet shade of half mourning were it not ostentatiously decorated with beads and lace. Nobody could have mistaken it for anything other than a ball gown.

And the gown's owner, though she was practically snarling, was beautiful. She was tall and fair, with deep blue eyes and golden hair. She had a complexion that could have been sickly were it not for the fact that her cheeks were pink, and she seemed quite healthy and strong.

"I'm sure that your place is not in the library, either," said Judith. "My name is Miss St Clair. I am the rector's daughter."

She should have added some polite niceties about the ball or about how she had come to find herself with a large collection of expensive books. But she was completely unwilling to make such a concession. She wanted just enough politesse to make the young woman feel ashamed and no more.

"Miss Haddington," said the young woman. She did not

include her first name, but Judith already knew her to be the wealthy family's only daughter. And of course she was. With a name like Louisa-Margaretta, she could only be a princess.

"Someone is coming in here," the young princess said, now hushed. "Hurry!"

She dragged Judith behind a curtain before she could explain then whispered to her, "It is only Aunt Matilda. But she will kill me if she discovers that I have left the ball. It was her chief aim that I survey all of the eligible gentlemen, particularly my own cousins, whom I could just as easily speak with across the breakfast table."

Judith only nodded, silenced by the revelation. She could not quite soothe her wounded feelings, not even upon hearing that Miss Haddington's aunt was equally interfering. Surely, that was no excuse for treating a guest so poorly. She looked away, out the window at the frozen ground. Judith had the sense that she was not truly meant to know anything about Miss Haddington or her cousins but that the urgency of the moment had led Louisa-Margaretta to speak to her almost as a friend.

The door to the library opened. It wanted oil. Judith reflected that the room might not get enough use for anyone to notice the problem with the door. It would not have surprised her to learn that all the Haddingtons and Ramsburys preferred either hunting or parties to reading. After all, Louisa-Margaretta did not appear to have her own book. The room was solely a sanctuary for her, its great wealth of volumes pearls before swine.

They heard the older woman's voice, the one who spoke with a Scottish inflection. She sounded just as merry as she had in the ballroom, but there was a softer note in her voice, too, one of affection.

"My darling, at last!"

There was a pause, and then she laughed. "Why, it is not

time for supper! Only, you have surprised me. Well. Stealing from the kitchens, I suppose, is its own gift. A bit early for Christmas cake, perhaps, but I will not refuse."

They heard the sound of the door again and someone eating and drinking. They could not be sure whether it was the same woman who had spoken before, but when Judith thought she detected snoring, Miss Haddington pulled at her arm again.

"She is asleep. We must hurry."

Miss Haddington kept such a grip on the lacy sleeve of Judith's gown that it seemed sure to tear. They were down the stairs and nearing the ballroom before Judith pulled away. "I do not see why we had to hide from your aunt," she said. "She would have scolded you for neglecting your duties as daughter of the hostess, I suppose."

"You suppose wrongly, Miss St Clair," said Miss Haddington, drawing herself up. "She would have lectured me, yes. But worse, she would have forced me to return and then complained to my mother. My aunt is no ally of mine, and she is already cross with me."

"I hardly think being scolded and forced to attend a party is a harsh punishment," said Judith, who only hours before had been on the verge of tears as her own aunt and sister attempted to do that very thing.

"Well, you know little of my family," said Miss Haddington. "And I wish you well. To be perfectly honest, if any of my eligible cousins tries to dance with you, it would be best for you to make any excuse you can and run away. They are bores, all three of them. Theo has a bit more wit than the others, but I have a feeling that he is the most boring in his heart, and I do not intend to find out by marrying him."

"Well, I say," said a gentleman of some fifty years, bumping into the pair of them. Judith recognized him as the man in the purple tailcoat they had seen earlier. Since he appeared close to the family without being a part of it, she wondered why he was attending the ball. And why he had slipped away.

And, of course, Judith was most worried about what this mysterious friend of the family might say about his discovery. In the heat of the argument, they had forgotten to watch the passage, and they needed to convince this gentleman that they had only been absent from the ball for a moment. Miss Haddington drew herself up again.

"Mr Bragg," she said, her face bursting into a smile that, while insincere, was indisputably beautiful. "Tell me, has supper been served? We were going to the kitchens to see when it might be ready and were waylaid by Miss St Clair's desire to see our beautiful breakfast room."

"Yes, quite something, what?" he said vaguely. "I wager your friend has never seen a finer."

He smiled at her, but as they had not been introduced, he could make no further comment. Miss Haddington did not seem to register this and stared absently at the man.

"Perhaps we should join the ball again, what?" he said. "Allow me to escort you, Miss Haddington."

The gentleman seemed to be lurching along in an odd manner. There had not been the smell of liquor on him, but it was possible he had already had far too much wine. Judith followed them back to the ballroom, wondering why her companion had not thought to make any introductions. Apparently, as soon as she stopped being in Miss Haddington's way, Judith was quite forgot.

But that did not mean she would forget what she had learned. Miss Haddington was an unpleasant sort, but her description of her cousins gave Judith pause. If even the closest family members of the three Mr Ramsburys could not recommend them, they must be very troublesome gentlemen indeed.

Judith felt dizzy from hunger and fatigue. After only hours in the house, she had nearly been found out in a most compromising position, and now surely, her family had done their duty by their patrons.

She would have to convince her papa to leave before supper.

6

When she returned to the ballroom, there were no signs that they would ever be presented with any food. She wondered whether Miss Haddington's lie would hold. In a house of this size, it would be strange to send the hostess's daughter to check on the meal when a servant would have managed it more quickly. But Mr Bragg seemed eager to re-establish his presence in the ballroom and to escape from Miss Haddington, who had been rattling on about game and poachers just as boldly as any young man of fashion.

Judith easily found her papa. He was speaking to a different elderly widow, but the subject was nearly the same. She wondered whether he had left off for even a moment. He was now speaking of the many miracles of the Christmas story and how it was easy to forget them when one heard the story year after year. Each one, to him, was like an insect preserved in amber, complete in its fascination and perfection.

"Papa," she said. "I believe we should be leaving. It would

be best for us to return home before the snow, in case the boys should need us."

"We are only down the lane," he said. "And your sister is dancing."

Judith started. He was correct. Miriam was finishing a quadrille, looking serious as she concentrated on the steps. Her dance partner was Mr Morgan Ramsbury, the young man who had barely spoken two words to them earlier in the evening.

Judith concluded that the young man's aunt, or perhaps his father, must have forced him to ask young ladies to dance. It would be impolite for him to simply stand in the ballroom, refusing to even speak with them. But she felt for her sister. Miriam would be taken in and would likely fancy herself in love with the first rich man who spoke two words to her. And in this case, Mr Morgan Ramsbury was hardly likely to speak more than two words.

She made another attempt to leave, but as the dance finished, the supper began.

It was only after the meal, when Judith had resigned herself to dancing with a man who appeared even less interested in the amusement than Mr Morgan Ramsbury, when they got the news. She was on the arm of Mr Fletcher, the eldest son of some neighbours or other, and he was going on about tithes in a manner so dull that even a young lady who depended on them was bound to feel sleepy.

Mrs Haddington had been the one to circulate most frequently amongst her guests, and Judith had run out of paths for avoiding her. But at one point, she left the room dragging Mr Ephraim Ramsbury, the rude physician, with her by his arm, and in his eyes, Judith noticed much more focus than she had observed when he was dancing. The pair of them did not return. It was Mr Haddington who addressed the room. And how he got everyone to fall silent, at a point in the evening when many glasses had been drained, Judith could not have said. His voice was clearer than she would have imagined. For the first time that evening, he did not mumble one bit.

"Friends," he began. "I'm sorry, but we need to end our festivities now. You need not visit the retiring room; the maids are on their way with your coats, and we will let the coachmen know. Goodnight."

Judith couldn't help thinking that their hostess would have explained things much more gracefully. A chorus of voices arose amongst the guests. Of those not in the family, there were perhaps only forty in total, but not one could account for the strange turn the evening had taken.

And then Judith's father was summoned.

❧ 7 ❧

It was the next morning before he told Miriam and Judith all that had passed. Breakfast was often a loud affair, but because their brothers only wanted to go out and play during the unusually sunny morning, they were clumsily dispatched while their father shared the news with the ladies of the household.

"They wished me to bless the late Miss Ross," he said. "She was a distant relation of Mrs Haddington, our hostess. Miss Ross's sister Sally, who married one of Mrs Haddington's brothers, is no longer living. Neither is Mr Noah Ramsbury, Mrs Haddington's brother, although his adopted son is with the party. I believe you met him last night, Judith, dear? Were the two of you dancing?"

Miriam nodded. "Yes, that glum fellow? Mr Ephraim Ramsbury? I danced with him, too, you know. He said that I had a good memory for the steps of the quadrille."

She smirked as she said it, but it was no more than the truth. Miriam had long been an excellent dancer, and only someone with a truly miraculous memory could have gone years without a dancing master and still managed to dance no fewer than six dances before the evening was cut short. Judith was relying on the couples who called the steps and on the memory her body seemed to retain of many such evenings and ballrooms, but since Miriam had never been out, she did not have this advantage.

"Miss Ross was hardly related to the family, then?" said Judith. It seemed strange that Louisa-Margaretta had referred to the lady as an aunt, since the sister of her mother's sister-in-law was not a very close kinship tie.

"Well," said Papa, looking tired. "She is the adopted aunt of Mr Ephraim Ramsbury, Mrs Haddington's nephew. So I suppose he must be the reason for her inclusion in the party. And from all I have heard, both Mrs Sally Ramsbury and Mr Noah Ramsbury were rather extraordinary people. They could not have children of their own and adopted none apart from Mr Ephraim Ramsbury, so now that they have both passed, he would be on his own each Christmas were it not for his more distant relations. I am sure that, as a widower, that would be lonely for him."

Judith winced. It was an unusually long speech for Papa, but he clearly felt for the bereft Mr Ephraim Ramsbury. Perhaps, in spite of the great differences between the two men, their shared status of widower was enough for sympathy to overcome station and inclination.

"Ought he to care for those children, do you think?" mused Aunt Leah. "With no woman to help him?"

Her thoughts had certainly gone along the same lines as Judith's, but Papa nodded as firmly as he could. "Mr Ephraim Ramsbury was himself sent to live with relatives when his own mother died," he said. "He was an only child, and his father found that he could not manage in his grief. He tells everyone that he has always resented his father for sending him away and that he would not wish such a thing on his own children."

Miriam was tapping her foot, more interested in the death that had occurred only the day before than the passing of Mr Ephraim Ramsbury's mother decades ago.

"I don't believe Mr Ephraim Ramsbury said two words to Miss Matilda Ross," said Miriam. "That particular gentleman seems to think himself far above his company, and even his adopted aunt could not interest him."

"He was not interested in the ball," said Judith, defending the man, though she could hardly say why. "I am not sure we ought to censure him for that."

Aunt Leah shook her head. "We needn't gossip," she said firmly. "Though I suppose we ought to find out what happened to her," she added, turning her worried face to her brother. "Should we worry for the girls?"

The look she gave their father was full of hidden import, but neither of the Misses St Clair was fooled. It was quite clear to them that she was thinking of their mother. If there was even a hint of contagion, it threatened not only their lives but the return of a grief that had overwhelmed all of them. Disease and sickbeds were to be avoided at all costs.

"Nothing of that sort, no," said the rector, spooning out far too much marmalade and looking distinctly uncomfortable. "She was not a danger to any of us, poor soul."

"Well, then," said Miriam. "I suppose you shall be in charge of the funeral, and soon?"

Their father only shook his head. "We did not speak of the arrangements. I am sure that shall fall to the family."

Judith and her aunt exchanged a look.

"Father," she said carefully. "You are the rector, and thus the individual in charge of such things. What is more, you already blessed the departed. Was she not a member of the church?"

"Oh, no," he said. "That is, I could not speak to that. But I believe she was."

Seeing that none of them would let him rest without an answer, he put down the piece of bread.

"This cannot be said outside our home," he told them. "Miss Ross took poison."

There was a shocked silence, but only for a moment.

Aunt Leah shook her head. "Well, if she took her own life, we can only pray that God will forgive her for a moment of madness."

"God may," Miriam murmured. "Society, however, certainly shall not."

It was an opinion none of the elder St Clairs could contradict.

❧ 8 ❧

They were to have a test of exactly how society would view the deceased woman no later than the breakfast hour, as it happened. They received a caller in the person of the dashing gentleman who had caught Miriam's eye the night before.

Indeed, Mr Theo Ramsbury's fine manners and looks had been remarked upon by every young lady and mama at the assembly, often in a rather crude and public fashion. He was the type of man who made every female on earth forget her age. Young girls not yet out cursed their youth and swooned over him as surely as they would were they close to him in age. Elderly gentlewomen made all sorts of speculation about what their relations would be with such a man if only they were "just a few years younger, my dear." Though his clothing was finely cut, Judith was certain that he would have made nearly the same impression were he a king or a labourer. That was simply part of his character.

He was not shown into the parlour but rather her father's study, where they stayed shut up for some time. When he left, though, Miriam rushed to the window to get a glimpse of him and blushed crimson when he turned back and tipped his hat to her with a smile.

"For shame, Miri," said Judith, more out of habit than actual feeling. "He is here to speak with Papa about a funeral. A rather difficult one, as it happens."

But she did not feel sorry the way she ought. Indeed, she had once thought that if she were ever to lose a member of her family, she would feel in her heart what others experienced when they went through the same trial.

Instead, it seemed to have hardened her. She believed that no other person could possibly feel the grief that she felt for her own mama. And while she knew this to be untrue, she had a great deal of trouble scolding her steady heart into sympathy. It was as if all of the reserves of grief and sorrow that were meant to last her a lifetime had been exhausted, and she would never be able to have even a drop of them back. She would have to play her part well if she was to avoid offending the Haddingtons.

Miriam was the one who rushed off to their father, bringing him into the little parlour to speak to them all about the visitor. Even though the rectory was much grander than their former home in Essex, Judith could not help seeing the room as diminutive after the immense spaces of the house where they had stayed until the small hours. And it would be strange for the younger son of a mere visitor to say anything about a funeral. What could have brought Mr Ramsbury from that fine house to pay a call on a man who, a week ago, was a complete stranger to him?

Miriam, it appeared, had the same question.

"What did he want, Papa?" she said. "And did he say anything about the dancing, or more particularly, about me?"

Their aunt had left, so she was not there to scold them, but even Judith recognized the impertinence.

"Miriam, please."

Her sister scowled and would have stuck out her tongue had she not been told that at the age of nineteen, this was considered unladylike.

"You wish to know just as much as I do."

"Yes, but there is no need to talk of the dancing. I am sure it was not the chief topic of conversation."

"No indeed," said their father. "In fact, his request was much less conventional, but I do hope to honour it."

Miriam and Judith waited, and when it became apparent that he was not about to say more, Miriam began to beg.

"We could help you with the request, Father! Is it about the burial? Because you know we always used to find Mr Mullens to give him news."

This was the truth. Drew Mullens, the gravedigger in the village of Greenhill, was known to all. Many called him simple, but he was kind, and children in particular always liked him. Miriam and Judith had often run to his mother's house to provide news after someone passed away. It was a kindness, and they felt the import of letting Mr Mullens get on with his work without any delay. They also knew a lady who would do the flowers, and they played almost daily with the children of the coffin maker.

In their new village, they had no such knowledge, and their ability to be useful after a death seemed much diminished.

"You may help, I suppose," he said thoughtfully. "I am to pay them a call this morning. And though I cannot reveal the private nature of the visit, I know their daughter might prefer your company to her elders'. She is, I believe, of a delicate constitution."

Judith very nearly snorted. The young woman she met yesterday had not seemed "delicate" in the least. Prone to fits of temper, perhaps, but certainly not weak. Then again, she reflected, there had certainly been something wrong about

Miss Haddington from the start. Judith had no doubt that the fiery temper she had seen was genuine, but there was a desperation in the young woman's look, a sense that she was somehow on edge. The purple beneath her eyes spoke to a lack of sleep, and how a young woman of means in a vast country house could manage not to sleep well Judith would never understand. Young ladies such as Miss Haddington could sleep early or late. Unlike Judith, Miss Haddington didn't have to contend with little brothers who escaped their beds to pester their sisters in the middle of the night.

No, when Miss Haddington spoke of the eligible gentlemen, there was something beyond simple annoyance. Judith wondered if there might have been a reason for the young woman to marry soon and to marry a member of her family at that.

With a flash, she started. She remembered various weddings that her father had performed which others would have dismissed as indecent. There was a term for them that her mother did not allow her to use. He was of a belief, one he could not have held more firmly had it been actually written in the Bible itself, that people who had come to the decision to marry should not be barred by societal conventions from accepting the institution created by God.

In practice, this meant some unions that were much talked of. Young widows with men who could have been grandfathers. Soldiers on their way to France, with only minutes to spare. And, of course, many brides whose children would bear the pride of legitimacy but who would not have such a claim had their mothers (and the men who married their mothers, for Judith was not naive enough to believe that these men were always the natural fathers) waited even a week longer.

Miss Haddington had not been sleeping. She seemed ill, and much as she wished to avoid choosing a husband from amongst her cousins, she seemed to regard such a thing as inevitable. Moreover, she was not thin like Judith but full-figured. Her gown was clearly new. Had it, perhaps, been specially designed to conceal a certain shape?

With understanding came a wave of remorse. Judith had made fun of a young woman who, if spoiled, was in a situation that no other young woman would envy. A situation that, very soon, would become impossible to conceal.

"I would be happy to accompany you, Papa," she said. "Miriam, shall we go and prepare? I am sure Papa will not wish to be kept waiting."

9

Their entrance to the grounds was very different in the early afternoon. The sunlight that had so delighted their brothers early in the day had passed, and the clouds seemed to make the grounds every bit as cold as they had been the day before.

In many ways, they were worse, as Judith no longer had any anticipation to warm her. Though she had railed against the ball, she had been interested in the Haddingtons in spite of herself. If what she felt the night before was mostly anger, it had still been enough to make her forget the cold for some moments. Now, she felt every bit of it. She wished she had eaten more at breakfast rather than begging her father for details of the sad death. Perhaps then she would not be shivering.

During the carriage ride, Miriam begged their father for details of his mission, and he refused. But as soon as they were welcomed into Wycliff Castle, Mrs Haddington appeared, full of apologies and quite determined to pile blessings upon them. She had no idea of secrecy and soon revealed that she had asked the rector to her home that he might bless the space where death had taken their dear Miss Ross.

"You are an angel to agree to it," she said. "Girls, your father is an angel. And after he finishes his blessing, we shall all pray for him."

Judith dared not look at Miriam. Though certain rather enthusiastic parishioners were, at times, likely to say they would pray for her father, the tone here seemed to be something entirely different. Mrs Haddington was pressing their arms, exclaiming with wide gestures, all while leading them skilfully down a hall.

"I know that it is a heathen custom in many ways," she said. "And I needn't burn the juniper, if you do not wish me to, Mr St Clair. But one cannot doubt that the room is impure, and I wish to give the library over to my daughter and let her remember her aunt with love."

That seemed to startle their papa just enough. "To speak of your daughter," he said. "I had hoped my own daughters might call on her, perhaps, while I fulfil your request?"

For the first time, Mrs Haddington was silent. "To tell the truth, I cannot say whether Louisa-Margaretta is awake. I went to her bed to pray with her this morning, and she was still sleeping quite soundly. But perhaps I should be able to find her with such charming company." She turned, then, pressing Judith's hand. "You can find your way, dear? Go to our little family sitting room, where you are sure to find at least one of the gentlemen. And from there, you may seek my daughter."

As soon as they were free of Mrs Haddington, Miriam began to complain. "I don't wish to speak to her! I want to see the library where it happened."

"Miriam! Suicide is a ghastly thing."

"It is not," Miriam responded. "And besides, we don't know that it was suicide. It could have been apoplexy. That can be very sudden. Or perhaps she knew she was dying, and she wanted to come to a very grand house for Christmas."

"The Christmas plans were rather hasty," murmured Judith. "The Haddingtons only just purchased Wycliff Castle. They have not been here a month. If she had any knowledge, it cannot have been long before."

"She did not look like a woman who was about to die," mused Miriam. "I thought she was going to dance every dance before she disappeared. I must say, it was rather indecent."

"They were respectable dances."

"Yes, but a quadrille, at her age? She cannot have been courting. She was more a spinster than anyone else at the ball, and yet her feet were flying."

"A spinster can still dance if she wishes," snapped Judith. "At any rate, if I thought this Christmas might be my last, I daresay I would have danced more myself, in spite of the temperament of the gentlemen who happened to attend."

Miriam gave a great sigh at this and shrugged her shoulders. They had only just passed the entrance. The house truly was palatial, and Judith looked about to make sure they were not overheard.

"Some of the gentlemen were quite agreeable," said Miriam. "And on the whole, it seems a strange night for such a cheerful woman to die. Perhaps she was murdered!"

"Miri," groaned Judith. Miriam meant no harm with her words, but she had not yet learned to be very careful with her speeches in such a grand house. There were family members across the place and likely servants in nearly every room. It was rumoured that Mr and Mrs Haddington had at least four dozen servants, some local but many who had come with them when they moved. Judith knew that she and her sister could not speak plainly about scandal the way they always could in their own home. Besides, either their aunt or their father would not have allowed such remarks.

Judith, it seemed, was fast losing whatever influence she had once held over her sister. And her timing was not perfect in that regard, because Miriam was now more vulnerable than ever.

This was evident in the warm greeting she gave Mr Ephraim Ramsbury, the dishevelled man who was the adopted son of Mr Noah Ramsbury, one of Mrs Haddington's brothers. At the ball, he had seemed presentable enough, but this morning, his hair and clothing were askew, though his manners were unchanged. He had been cold to them the night before and remained cold in the morning, but Miriam either did not notice or wisely pretended that he had shown much better breeding.

"These must be your dear children," she said, settling herself before the fireside with two girls. Both were younger than she was, but Miriam still looked far less out of place in that scene than she had at the ball. To think she was interested in marrying their papa, when she was hardly out of the nursery herself.

"I suppose their governess has her half day today, Mr Ramsbury?" Judith asked, hoping to deflect some of the attention from her sister. Though she had no wish to court such a disagreeable gentleman, she did not want Miriam to form any expectations.

His face soured. "They do not have a governess. I see to their education myself."

She raised her eyebrows. "That is singular." She could not help looking about the room at the rich decorations and furnishings. These two daughters, whom Mr Ramsbury had introduced as Anna and Agnes, were surely the only young girls in the country who inhabited such fine rooms without the benefit of a governess.

"So, although I do not have any particularly useful occupation at the moment, I should hand my children's education over to others? I would much prefer to do it myself."

She held her hands up, wondering how soon she could escape the room. "I understand. We had no governess and got all of our own education from our parents. Only, I understand that in certain circles, this is less usual."

She thought she saw his face grow a bit less sour, though she might have imagined it in the hazy light of the afternoon. "Yes. Quite."

Finding no joy in her conversation with Mr Ramsbury, who looked even older than he had when he was attempting to dance with a series of young ladies, Judith moved over to the fire. Miriam was playing with an old card that held some remnants of lace, already finding the children's games tedious but determined to be polite. Judith listened to the two of them squabbling.

"We can't eat the pudding on Christmas," said Agnes. "It might be poisoned."

"No, it isn't poisoned," said Anna. "Because we all made it together, and Cook let me taste all the ingredients."

Both looked to be about the age of ten, but it was the younger one, Anna, who was most intent on the poison theory.

"We will light it on fire, and it will be poison, and we shall all die," she said, falling over for dramatic effect.

Judith looked to their father for help, but he was staring out the window as if he might force the sun to emerge by staring at it. She could tell he was not hearing anything of what his daughters said, and she became curious.

"Why do you speak of poison?" she asked. When the older one hesitated, Judith tried to make her question more innocent. "Is it part of a game?"

"No," said Anna, suddenly serious. "Our auntie died

because she ate poison cake. But we ate it, too, and we didn't die."

"Our slices weren't poisoned," murmured Agnes, clearly embarrassed to be in the position of explaining these rather simple facts to her younger sister. "That is why we did not die. If they did have the same poison, we would have died more quickly, because we are smaller."

Miriam had put down the card of lace. She did not look scared, but she was staring at the two girls. However many conversations of this nature Judith and Miriam had in private, they always knew better than to have them in front of their father.

But the father, in this instance, was still staring at shadows. He appeared not the least bit concerned by all this talk of murder.

"Pardon me," said Judith. "Mrs Haddington requested that I find her daughter. Could you tell me where Miss Haddington might be at this hour?"

"On her way to go ride," said a figure in the doorway. "Only Mama forgot to bring my best riding habit, and so I shall have to wear something else, I suppose."

"If it is not terribly troublesome to you, might you find one for me?" ventured Judith. "I would appreciate the opportunity to join you."

And before either Miss Haddington or Miriam could object, she left the room.

10

The smell of juniper grew stronger as soon as they entered the entrance hall. It wasn't proper to leave Miriam alone with Mr Ephraim Ramsbury and the children, but Judith decided that she could hardly be expected to play chaperone for the whole morning. Besides, provided nobody cared about appearances, the thought of Miriam and the older physician being in any romantic danger was laughable. There was a possibility that Mr Ephraim Ramsbury was their poisoner, but Judith discounted it. He would have had no reason to poison his aunt, and even if he were guilty, he would hardly attempt more violence within sight of his inquisitive, beloved daughters.

Still, were she to be discovered, Judith would certainly be ordered either back into her sister's company or back to the rectory. She hoped that Mrs Haddington's religious fervour would keep her father occupied for at least ten more minutes, though she had always thought of burning herbs like juniper as a heathen practice. It was a fine thing that the wise rector was so tolerant of different traditions, provided he could read his own selections from the Old Testament as he performed them. Judith needed time to find a riding habit, and once she was wearing one, Papa could hardly tell her to insult Miss Haddington by going home. He would have to allow her a ride, even if he did not consider it suitable for a house in mourning. Besides, it was not a very long walk to the edge of the park and down the lane to the rectory. If she needed it, she could probably have a groom come with her, and that way, she could dismount at her own front door.

"Are you sure that you wish to ride?" asked Miss Haddington, hardly bothering to look at her. "I am sure the weather looks foul, and you are so thin. I would not wish for you to catch a chill."

"I am stronger than I look, thank you," said Judith curtly, and those were the last words they said to each other before they were both mounted and leaving the stables behind them.

Judith could not have said whether it was Miss Haddington's rudeness that kept her quiet. Perhaps the other young woman did have some sense of danger. As they neared the hills, Judith found that she was already struggling to keep up, holding tight to the saddle as she urged her little mare through the brambles and empty trees. When she finally drew up to Miss Haddington, she had to speak.

"Your aunt was poisoned," said Judith, feeling weary from all the time that she had spent holding her tongue.

"Yes," said Louisa-Margaretta. "She poisoned herself, poor fool. It was not enough for her to make my life miserable; she had to go and ruin Christmas for her entire family. She must have delighted in causing so much guilt. Every moment of the morning, Mama has been going on about what she should have seen and how she was so occupied with the ball, and now there is another angel. And all that."

She stopped herself, and Judith was not sure if it was because she was sick of talking or because she had finally remembered that her companion was a rector's daughter.

Judith suspected the former. Miss Haddington was already starting to spur her mount to a pace that did not feel comfortable to Judith.

"I'm trying to warn you," she said. "If my own sister noticed, others will have as well. Your aunt did not seem like a woman who was about to kill herself."

"She delighted in driving me to madness, but she was not mad herself? That is your proposition?"

"If you'll forgive me, Miss Haddington, you do not appear to be mad," said Judith drily. "Although I do wish you would allow your pace to slacken a bit, for my sake."

"I hide it well," said her companion bitterly, and they rode on at what seemed only a hair slower than the pace that Louisa-Margaretta had hurled her mount into previously.

"Miriam thinks that your aunt was murdered, and so do your young cousins," Judith said, and when she got only a laugh in return, she pressed on. "If the food that she was given was poisoned, but she did not know, then we were the last people to hear her speak."

"Who gave her the food?"

Judith looked over at Miss Haddington, so elegant in her seat but with a frown that could have rivalled any demon's.

"She is your aunt! Surely you know. I would not have recognized the voice."

"I don't believe the other person spoke," said Miss Haddington, and for the first time, she did slow down, although her pace was still too fast for Judith to be comfortable. "She spoke to him, surely."

"Him or her?"

"Him, certainly. From her tone, and from the fact that he was bringing her cake in the library. I wonder why he did not stay."

"Perhaps he did."

"If he did," she said slowly, "I would have seen him when we went out. No, he did not stay."

"Mr Bragg," said Judith. "Could he have gone in then left? We saw him moments later."

Louisa-Margaretta shook her head. "He would have no reason to wish any of us ill," she said. "He is not even part of our family."

Judith cleared her throat. "I wonder that he has chosen to spend Christmas with you, then."

"Mama likes to invite everyone on earth," said Louisa-Margaretta. "You probably noticed that the ball included most of the village as well as the neighbors."

But she spoke without her customary confidence.

The two of them rode along, neither daring to ask the next question that their conversation demanded. If not Mr Bragg, it must surely have been a member of the family, as Miss Ross was not on familiar terms with any of the guests at the ball. Judith was thankful for the shadow of the woods, for the protection that she had not felt when she was in the grand house. There, anyone could be listening. In the woods, they could be certain that nobody would hear of their conversation.

"It is ridiculous," said Miss Haddington, her voice full of doubt. "Why would any of our guests have wanted to kill her?"

Judith found that, all at once, she was able to speak honestly with Miss Haddington.

"To be quite frank, it sounds as if you did."

Instead of flouncing on, offended, Miss Haddington only shook her head. "I have my reasons. But I never would have poisoned her, anyway. I would have wanted to make her suffer, but I never would have wished for her death."

"Could it have been anything that happened on her visit? Perhaps she angered someone or bragged about her jewels?"

Louisa-Margaretta glared. "How do you know about her jewels?"

Judith sighed. "I know nothing about her jewels, but it seems as if she were a very wealthy woman, and such women often spend a great deal of money on specially set little pebbles because it makes them forget that their lives are empty."

She regretted what she had said, but Miss Haddington looked impressed for the first time. "Let me enlighten you on that point. My aunt was not wealthy, and we still have all of her pebbles, as you call them."

"I am sorry," murmured Judith, already regretting her outburst.

Louisa-Margaretta only laughed. "Pebbles, indeed! My, my, the rector's daughter with a criticism of her fellow man!"

"It was not a criticism," said Judith hastily. "But can you think of anything apart from the ordinary? Was there anything she did that was strange?"

"Apart from telling Mama to buy a ghastly old country house in the middle of a mountainous wilderness and thereby forcing me to spend Christmas there with three supposedly eligible cousins? No, I confess that I had not thought of anything else out of the ordinary."

Judith judged it best not to respond. If she had been quick to guess the reason for Miss Haddington's fast and shameful intended engagement, others must also know. The least she could do was feign ignorance for the moment, or perhaps forever.

"She was eating something that was brought to her," said Judith. "Supper had not been served."

"And you think that it was poisoned?"

"Yes."

They rode on. Miss Haddington was silent, and the scowl vanished from her face. "Well, I would not have wished that on her," she said. "But even if it is true, we'll never prove it."

"We must."

"I see no reason for that."

"Then you are a fool," said Judith, ignoring the gasp of outrage that burst from the other woman. "The person who killed your aunt? If he comes to realize that we were in the library and could have seen him, he may very well kill us next."

Miss Haddington needed no more convincing. She was stubborn, but she was not stupid, and she knew that the two of them might be in danger. But in her view, it was one of the new servants who had murdered her aunt, a party guest, or an outsider who had used a false name at the door.

Judith held firm. It was one of the people present at the ball and most likely one of the family.

Before the two of them reached the stables, Judith insisted that she was going to go about finding the murderer in her own way. She would examine the room, the family, and the servants. But she would be most careful when speaking to the family, because she saw no reason for a servant to suddenly take against a woman who was nearly unconnected to them. And the way that the murdered woman had spoken was hardly the tone she would have taken with a servant, or a stranger for that matter.

Miss Haddington refused. "I shall learn more about my aunt and see who it was," she said. "Perhaps it was a jilted lover."

"I hardly think a jilted lover would secretly come to a small gathering in Derbyshire to kill a respectable woman."

"Perhaps their love was an old one," said Miss Haddington. "And they could not marry, but they promised to love no other. And then, in a fit of selfishness, she betrayed him and married another. And years later, sick with jealousy, he killed her."

"I cannot imagine such a thing happening to anyone, let alone your aunt."

"Poppycock," said Miss Haddington sharply, and Judith flinched at the word. She had only ever heard it used by men, and then only rarely.

"I can imagine it very well," Miss Haddington continued. "Indeed, it is the only decent reason I can think of for murdering anyone, especially a woman of means and understanding."

Judith sighed. She had known little of murder in her lifetime, and when a person was killed, in her experience, it was usually a wife with a brute of a husband. In most cases, he would go unpunished unless someone in the woman's circle was equally rash and violent.

But she was also well aware that most people would think of money as one of the first reasons for a murder. Indeed, though she had no murderous intentions herself, money was never far from her mind. When some people starved and others had storerooms of every fine food, not to mention well-appointed horses and expensive riding habits, it was not hard to understand this. But she believed that Miss Haddington had never had to spare a thought for something so sordid as money, and so she imagined that every crime must be a crime passionnel.

The wood thinned again as they came within sight of the stables. Soon, they would no longer be able to speak of murder.

Judith fished about in her pockets until she found it.

"Here, take my mourning brooch."

"I do not intend to go so far for only an aunt."

Judith tried to control her glare. It was well known that the amount of time one mourned for an aunt was based on the strength of one's love and devotion, not some simple ritual. She wished she did not have to give her own precious mourning brooch to someone so entirely lacking in regard for the dead.

And yet her own lack of regard for the young Miss Haddington was precisely what would throw suspicion on her should she choose to return. It was going to be difficult to lie to her family about the true purpose of the visit. Aunt Leah, in particular, would see through it if she tried to pretend a new devoted friendship. She had never been easy around the likes of Miss Haddington in the past, had always insisted that wealthy young women were not worth her time. When her father argued Christian forgiveness, she insisted that she was not going to help a camel enter the eye of the needle when there were other friends who had greater sense and much better manners. So it was essential that she lose something. And because she had few possessions, the brooch was the best choice.

"If you need me, say that you have found a brooch that you think may be mine," she said. "But claim that you are not sure, and send for me so I can come and see it. That is how I will know you are serious."

"I am quite sure they shall catch the servant who did it," said Miss Haddington, though she did not look particularly sure. If Judith were a gambler, she would have laid money on the young lady having absolutely no idea about the running of the household. She likely did not know her servants' names, let alone what grudge they might hold against one of her family. The princess of the house probably did not know which servants had been with them for years and which were newly hired. It might put them at a disadvantage were they to need information.

The wind blew colder again as they approached the house, and she looked at Miss Haddington with a new pang of concern.

"I daresay I shall have news for you first," she said. "But until then, take care."

Mis Haddington scoffed. "I should be the one telling you to take care. You do not know how to shoot."

Judith felt the truth of that, but she hardly thought having a gun would be protection enough. After all, even swords were no longer permitted in polite company. "You are the one living under the same roof as a murderer."

12

"We are all to be living under the same roof for some time," said Louisa-Margaretta's mama, fluttering around the room the following morning. "So it is imperative that you come to breakfast, my dear. It is our sacred duty to make our guests welcome for as long as they are with us. The ball was a sad event, but it would not excuse a lapse of manners."

Louisa-Margaretta reflected that her mother did not seem at all sad. If anything, she was speaking of God with even more reverence, heading from one room to the next to share her revelations with all who would pretend to listen. And because she was the hostess, wife, or employer of everyone in the house, they all listened to her with rapturous attention.

All except her wayward daughter, who was burying herself under her blankets again. The last thing she wanted was breakfast with her cousins. Even an actress with years on the boards would have struggled with the displays of delicacy and emotion that Mama expected. To feign interest in Napoleon was difficult enough. To feign interest in her cousins, all of whom had the means to marry? Their lack of interest in her had to be genuine, because there was enough money on both sides to make all of the matches eligible, even desirable. No, simpering at any of those three men would be impossible.

And to make matters worse, her head, her stomach, and every sinew in her body seemed to be complaining. She wished she could have said it was all from the ride of the previous day, but she knew there was another cause.

"My dear," said Mama, sitting on top of the bed. Louisa-Margaretta felt the weight of her and could see her mother's expression in her mind, though she did not bother to lift the bedclothes. Mama would surely be looking nearly overjoyed, her faith and devotion dampened only slightly by her disobedient daughter. "You have been out for a decade now. Surely you realize that you are as much of a hostess as I am. More so, perhaps, because you can make the young men feel truly at ease."

"No," said Louisa-Margaretta, shuddering at the thought of making her cousins feel "at ease" in her house.

"Yes, my sweet," answered her mother without thinking. "Shall we take the night of the ball? After the third dance, you disappeared, and I had no idea where you had gone. Wilkins said you were not in your room, nor anywhere else that I had her check."

At this, Louisa-Margaretta raised the bedclothes immediately. "What, you sent your maid after me?"

Harriet, Louisa-Margaretta's maid, was young and as forgetful as she was eager to please. Wilkins, though, had been lady's maid to Mama for decades. Unlike Harriet, Wilkins missed nothing, and she would naturally have passed any suspicions on to her employer.

"As I said, dear, you were to be a sort of second hostess. And you would have had time to dance with many more of our guests had you not disappeared. The two Fletcher boys, in particular, both asked after you. Where did you go, dearest?"

Louisa-Margaretta nearly said that she was not about to give away a hiding place that had clearly been successful but stopped herself. Though she instinctively felt safe with her mother, she knew she could tell nobody.

"I wandered about," she said carefully. "I was in the parlour for some time and then the breakfast room. I came back to my room for a handkerchief, but I was not here long."

"I see," said her mama, smiling again. But Louisa-Margaretta knew that her mother would be suspicious. After all, Louisa-Margaretta's lies about her thoughts, feelings, and whereabouts were the cause of their sudden removal to this horrid place. Her time in Wycliff Castle could be thought of as a sort of prison sentence. Things that she used to do regularly, like riding alone and writing her own letters, were now closely scrutinized. She knew for certain that she had only been permitted to ride yesterday because Miss St Clair was with her.

And Miss St Clair, though she appeared every inch the poor and pious rector's daughter, had known how to divert suspicion. She had even thought of the mourning brooch now hidden in Louisa-Margaretta's neglected work basket.

The woman was useful for something, then, Louisa-Margaretta had to concede. If they were going to keep the truth from her mama, they would need all of the subterfuge they could summon.

"I've laid out your dress myself," said her mother. "I don't know why Harriet had that blue one ready for you."

"Because I asked her for it," she said. "Honestly, Mama, must we all go into mourning? It was only Aunt Matilda."

Her mother raised her eyebrows. "Not long ago, you were asking to wear mourning for a while yourself, my dear."

"That was not the same. It had to do with my vow never to marry, one that you have been determined to disrespect."

"I do not respect it because you will not either, my dear. You will wish to marry, and it is better that you do so now, before you gain the sort of reputation that will make it much more difficult."

Louisa-Margaretta could not dispute the truth of her mother's remarks. So she did not argue. She knew that there were already many men of the "best" families who would never marry her, and doubtless more would follow in that resolution. That is, if Miss St Clair was right and there had just been a murder in their home.

"I will always be able to marry if I choose. Only, I would prefer not to."

Mama did not quite look severe, more unaccountably serious. "You should not think you will always have the opportunity."

"You and Papa will always wish me married, and you will throw money at any suitor who will take me. So I shall never encounter any real difficulties."

Mama frowned, but she did not have anything to say on this point. The mercenary nature of her own marriage was a matter of public comment, certainly no secret even in Derbyshire.

"What you do not precisely understand, my dear," she said, "is this. The marriage you were proposing would not be a marriage in the eyes of God."

"So then, all people who do not belong to our church, they are all unmarried in His eyes? All heathens, their children bastards? I cannot believe this. Why, you are speaking of most of the children on earth, most of the people who have ever lived, whatever their views on marriage!"

If she thought this would put her mother off, she was

much mistaken. Rather, she had seized on one of her mother's favourite subjects.

"The question of the heathens, my dear," she said. "That is another thing entirely. Although, as we read in *Fordyce's Sermons*, it is not as if they did not have any wisdom at all. That is certain. However, one cannot possibly compare —"

"Mother," said Louisa-Margaretta. "Please pass me the black dress and call for Harriet. If you wish me to wear mourning today, I shall."

Harriet would come in, and her mother would leave. Louisa-Margaretta could not afford to spend all morning debating the fate of ancient heathen souls.

She would wear a hideous dress because that would suit her purposes. She had work to do.

13

Louisa-Margaretta tried the schoolroom first. It was a queer room, as it had never before been used for the education of children or for anything, really. And so it held the items they had bought with the house and then removed from other rooms, along with a smattering of books for Agnes and Anna. There were chairs that did not match and little end tables and a rather impressive collection of snuff boxes. Louisa-Margaretta wondered what had become of the family who used to own all these fine things, who had sold many of their possessions along with their home. What sort of life were they living now?

As someone who had been asked to abruptly give up many of her possessions and all of her friends, Louisa-Margaretta felt that her own situation was perhaps even more pitiable. Even if she had sworn off the idea of matrimony, she felt strongly that she ought not to be kept hidden in Derbyshire, where a ball was just an excuse for her to dance with her own cousins and the rather drunk nephew of a neighbour who did not live particularly near. When she thought of the life she had given up in town and in the country, her beloved was a part of it, but there were many other things that she missed. Surely, the family who had owned this house, even if they were living in penury, was able to find a great deal more amusement.

With a sigh, she went out to the garden, where she found the children at last.

"Are we wearing black, like the black cardinals, Papa?" asked Anna, running about in the garden.

Her sister Agnes was always more thoughtful. "We aren't like black cardinals," she said. "We can never be priests. Only a gentleman can be a man of the cloth."

"You can be nuns if you like," their father said, and Louisa-Margaretta was surprised to hear how gentle his voice was. She usually only spoke with him in company, and after dinner, she saw him scowl and complain about the frivolity of everything in sight.

"Why can't I be a black cardinal?" Anna said.

"My dear," he said. "I hope very much that you would be a black cardinal if you were asked to lie about an evil man's marriage and help him betray his wife."

Louisa-Margaretta frowned as she approached them. The last thing she wanted to speak of was Napoleon, and she wondered why Cousin Ephraim's young daughters were interested in the Corsican devil's affairs. Though she had managed an escape from the dreary conversations of the breakfast table, Napoleon's name was inescapable. When she was younger, she never spoke of politics, and yet her young cousins were shockingly well informed. At least, Agnes was. Anna had learned a few facts, which she now repeated to the tune of a nursery rhyme as she looked for holly berries. She added many of her own words and ideas, smiling as she went.

"Annulment is a sham, annulment is a sham, Taffy came to my house and stole a leg of lamb. I went to Taffy's house, and I stole Taffy's jam."

"There are reasons to annul a marriage, though," Louisa-Margaretta could not keep herself from adding. "It happens, if not daily, often. Though, of course, it is different with the Catholics."

"It is no different," said Cousin Ephraim, the customary anger that she was so used to hearing in his voice creeping back in. "It is a way for the people involved to avoid responsibility without the stain of divorce, and it is only a measure open to the rich."

"But surely, if they are avoiding divorce, there is some benefit to that?"

He sighed. "Who has neglected your education, cousin? Materially, there is no difference. In practice, both things are generally thought up by selfish men who do not wish to be dutiful to one wife but do not want to be jailed for bigamy, either."

She blinked. "And our own King Henry VIII?"

He laughed. "One of the worst offenders! Devise a new religion rather than doing one's duty by one's spouse. Shameful. Or shameless, rather."

For the first time, Louisa-Margaretta felt some interest in Cousin Ephraim. Since he had been widowed, she had seen almost nothing of him, and even during this visit, he had spent most of his hours caring for his daughters. But she held the idea of marriage, especially one made for love, as sacrosanct.

It was why she herself would never marry. She couldn't marry the man she loved, so it stood to reason that she could marry no other. And she couldn't become too friendly with her cousin, either, or she might give him useless ideas about her own intentions. If she told him the truth, that she had very nearly defied her family and married a Jewish man who still had her unswerving devotion, he would not be the least bit interested in her. But Mama refused to speak the whole truth, even with family, so Cousin Ephraim likely did not know all the details of the Haddingtons' sudden flight.

"I am also wearing black," Louisa-Margaretta said to Anna, hoping to draw the conversation away from marriage. "But I do not wish to be called a black cardinal. Ladies can wear black and be very elegant, can we not?"

Anna frowned. "How long must we wear it? I wanted to wear my best gown on Christmas and Boxing Day."

Louisa-Margaretta looked to the child's father. Since she had not intended to go into mourning at all, she had no idea what he wished for his children. She had seen the way that Judith flinched when Louisa-Margaretta said she did not wish to mourn Aunt Matilda for long. Though she still felt perfectly justified in that sentiment, she was more careful around the children.

"Your aunt has left us," Cousin Ephraim said. "So we must be in mourning at least until Christmas."

Anna opened her mouth to protest.

"We will settle it on Christmas Eve," he said.

"But Papa —"

"Anna. Is today Christmas Eve?"

"No."

"Very well. We will not speak of it until then."

Even Agnes looked rather shocked, but she did not contradict her father. Instead, she started her own search for holly berries, as Anna had not gathered very many.

Louisa-Margaretta looked down at her own drab mourning dress. It had been pretty enough when it was commissioned, upon the death of her grandmother, but she had grown at least two inches since then, and even though Wilkins had helped Harriet with the alterations, it fitted poorly at best. Anna appeared too fair and too tall for her own mourning gown, which looked babyish even for a child of her age, and Louisa-Margaretta felt how horrid it was for a child to be deprived of her Christmas finery. It put her in mind of her mother's cousin Martha's story about the fire in their London house. Martha had all of her new clothes just made, since she was twelve and growing quickly, and after the fire, nobody could spare a thought for her. Her great-grandmother was the only person to bother, but that grand old lady's tastes were quite different, and she took Martha off to the shops and ordered gowns that were thirty years out of fashion, heavy, and uncomfortable. Martha's treasured new clothes had all been lost, so she went about dressed like a miniature dowager.

"I have a lovely book about Christmas," she said to Agnes and Anna. "Perhaps we can read about it, and that will make the time go more quickly."

Agnes's father frowned. "I did not know you were a great reader, cousin."

Louisa-Margaretta rolled her eyes. Apart from romantic novels, which she had to hide from her mother, she was not a keen reader. But she had another motive.

"Come, children," she said. "Let us go and see the library."

14

When Louisa-Margaretta entered the library with Agnes and Anna, she very nearly coughed. Somehow, her mother had talked that gullible vicar into using juniper, and the room was redolent with the odour. It remained a mystery to Louisa-Margaretta why her mother stayed with the church, when clearly, she ought to have been some sort of heathen. Mama loved the changes of the seasons and the ancient rituals with a sort of madness, and only her eagerness to accept the church's dubious transformations of these rituals (Green boughs for the birth of the Christ child! Fertility symbols for His resurrection!) kept her from seeing that she was embracing a religion that was not at all in keeping with her natural inclination.

Agnes settled into a chair at once with a volume of her own choosing. Anna, who had clearly never been allowed in this library before, was occupied at once. She pulled all sorts of volumes from the shelves while Louisa-Margaretta went over the details of the room.

The furniture was mostly as she remembered, though her aunt's chair had been pulled up so near to the fire she wondered how it wasn't singed and why neither her mama nor the rector had disturbed the queer tableau. There was another chair that was closer to the fire than she had remembered, though she was certain that her aunt had been left alone. It was strange, she reflected, that not a single housemaid had been in to tidy the room. Perhaps they were all too superstitious. There were still errant crumbs on the floor. Louisa-Margaretta, though she had the appetite of a boy of thirteen and never heeded her governess's strict instructions to eat more "ladylike" portions, still would not have spilled so many crumbs. For the first time, she wondered at her aunt's state of mind.

There was a book on the chair that ought to have provided more information, but she could not say how. It was *The Law's Disposal of a Person's Estate Who Dies with No Will or Testament*, which she thought would hardly be her aunt's preferred reading. In fact, Aunt Matilda hardly read anything at all. Mr Ephraim Ramsbury was always reading with his two daughters, and Mr Morgan Ramsbury was a great reader himself, but other than that, she could not think of a single person in the family who had a great enjoyment of books. Her father liked the occasional cheap novel full of violence and drama, though he knew that her mother disapproved. Her mother's readings were almost purely theological.

"Cousin Louisa-Margaretta," said Anna. "Is there a book of maps up there? I should like to read about Rome."

"A book of maps will not tell you a great deal," said Louisa-Margaretta, obligingly standing on her own tiptoes to bring down an atlas. "But you may as well borrow this one. Mind, it is years out of date. I used it in the schoolroom."

She sensed someone coming down the passage, and she had still not achieved her aim.

The Bible was not the book that she sought. Besides, she ought to have had her own, had she not given it to her mother to give to some "poor souls" who had damaged theirs. This act of "charity" had been giving her an excuse for not reading the Bible each night. Still, Louisa-Margaretta took the first one she found and put it in a pile between more atlases. It was the only book that she could read openly without arousing suspicion, though she knew that if anyone actually noticed she was reading it, they would wish to try to engage her in some tedious discussion of the Divine.

That was not her wish at all.

"Come, cousin," she said. "It is time we returned these books to the schoolroom and found your father."

When they passed Cousin Morgan in the passage, she gave him a wide smile and a cheerful greeting so that he would not be too curious about the books. She walked ahead of her little cousins then turned to hurry them along just in time to see Cousin Morgan enter the library.

The next morning, the household was the picture of distraction, with each inhabitant lost in his own thoughts, leaving plenty of time for reading. Louisa-Margaretta had been urged to study her Bible many times but never with murder in mind. When she read through stories that had once been familiar, this time in search of ideas on that subject, she received quite an education. She learned, upon other things, that money appeared to be a powerful motivator. Indeed, it seemed that men would kill for it. In this aspect, at least, the impertinent Miss St Clair had (perhaps) been correct.

It was incomprehensible to Louisa-Margaretta. Having grown up in a wealthy family, she had never understood why anyone would be obsessed with money. Of course, she could also not imagine being without money. Her father, in his way, had tried to teach her. He did become upset when she was careless with something that was expensive, like gold thread ("We can get it easily in the shops, Papa") or silk shoes. But he also insisted that she have the best of everything.

Her mother, on the other hand, thought all talk of money unseemly. Each time Louisa-Margaretta raised the subject, her mother changed it to another. Her father was the opposite, more than ready to speak about his coffers and his business, but because his dear wife disallowed such talk in Louisa-Margaretta's presence, he always obeyed this directive. The result was that his daughter, though well schooled in needlework and drawing room etiquette, had not ever had the benefit of what she reasoned must be some rather impressive experience. After all, though she knew little of the particulars, she did know that her family's holdings grew grander with each passing year and that she had been much sought after in her first season because of both her beauty and her purse.

She allowed herself a thought of the season that had just ended, by far the most passionate and most disappointing of all her many seasons in the haut ton. She had tried not to linger over the pages of Song of Solomon, but the knowledge that her beloved Isaac read the same lines (in Hebrew, no less!) tantalized her. She found herself torn between a certainty that he still loved her and a dark belief that she would never see him again. Her parents had been quite clear that no letters of hers would ever be allowed to pass through the village and that if she found a servant to help her, they would let that person go immediately without pay or a reference. She knew that his parents were hardly likely to take a view that was any more charitable. When she had asked Isaac, he had been quite firm. Any future bride of his needed to be Jewish, at least according to his family. Louisa-Margaretta's mother insisted that she marry a man who shared their faith, though to give her a very small bit of credit, she was equally opposed to Jewish, Catholic, and nonbelieving men. The man's actual beliefs mattered little if he did not fulfil the basic requirements that, to Louisa-

Margaretta's parents, were absolutely necessary for the happiness and social position of their only daughter.

Louisa-Margaretta, though she knew little of money, knew just enough to realize that she could not ask a servant to risk their livelihood for her. She had no objection to doing so but considered it an impractical route. In fact, she had already tried, with Harriet, and been roundly scolded by both her parents. Any other attempts would be fruitless. Doubtless they were all gossiping about the one she had made in the servants' hall, and even the most naive little scullery maid was sure to be on her guard.

Louisa-Margaretta had known an exalted love, one that other mortals might dream about for their entire lives. Yet with her exile and her aunt's murder, this fact was no longer quite enough to steady her in these times. What would Isaac say about her current predicament, she wondered? She longed to know.

She found herself at the window, staring at the grand entrance to the house. Her cousin Morgan was coming down the drive, perhaps returning from another of his interminable walks. He seemed far too thin to survive such cold, but he walked quickly and never seemed to shiver. Her mother was also returning through the same entrance after having been to the village on yet another mission of charity and godliness. A death in the family would not stop her from thinking herself the saviour of the poor.

In London, her mother had often walked with a wide smile through the most dreadful neighbourhoods, just as fearless as she was fashionable. Louisa-Margaretta's father thought her charity visits mad and tried to convince her to sit at home and take up needlework. To his credit, he did not stop her going, although Louisa-Margaretta wondered if that would have been possible. Her mama was not a woman who was easily put off, as evidenced by her walk through the cold, which was neither slow nor hurried. She could have taken one of the carriages or at least a horse, but instead, she would stride about in thick boots like a pauper.

She saw Morgan catch sight of her mother, pretend not to have seen her, and stride off quickly in the other direction.

Louisa-Margaretta, fascinated, closed her Bible. This was not the first time she had seen the younger Mr Ramsbury avoid her mother, though it was the most obvious.

She recalled that he had been doing the same with their aunt, who was now deceased. There were several times that Aunt Matilda tried to speak to him. In fact, at one point, she had made mention of a "meeting" that she was sure Morgan had attended in Bath. There was a twinkle in her eye when she spoke of it, but her nephew had made his excuses and got away before she could explain.

And now, Aunt Matilda was dead, and nobody would ever be able to ask her what "meeting" she had in mind when she challenged Cousin Morgan. He was a quiet man, to be sure, but perhaps his reticence masked some sort of criminality. It put Louisa-Margaretta in mind of a Mr Audley, a notorious man in the London clubs that her brother Percival liked to frequent. Mr Audley gave every appearance of being a shy man, perhaps a bit foolish, waving money about and misunderstanding the rules at every table.

And at the end of the evening, he had bumbled his way into a small fortune by cheating. Percival always bragged that he was sure he would see Mr Audley die in a duel one day, though that was one of the few comments that tended to get a sharp response from their mama.

Mrs Haddington did not approve of duelling, nor did she approve of jokes about duelling. She would be happy to read the most grisly passages from scripture at any time, but acknowledging the darker realities of Percival's set was not something she enjoyed. She had even tried to reform him by visiting and forcing him to spend more hours with his charming wife, Peggy. And it might have been interesting to see if such a determined mother could ever mend the chasm that had sprung up between the two of them. But Louisa-Margaretta's situation had distracted her, and now, Percival was surely back to his wild ways at all the clubs and in the army.

Louisa-Margaretta gave a small smile, trying to cover her shock. There were black sheep in her family, to be sure — Percival was one, she was another. But she never would have believed that one of them was a murderer. She was very sorry to have been taken in by her cousin Morgan but glad that she had been able to observe him. It was time to send the mourning brooch back to Miss St Clair.

❧ 16 ❧

Judith very nearly clung to her father's coat when he left, and that alone should have made him suspicious.

Since she was a little girl, visiting her father's parishioners had been considered one of her principal duties. And she had always hated it, especially when she was very young. How they would pinch her cheeks and try to offer her refreshment that she had no interest in eating! When Miriam and her brothers began coming on the visits, in many ways, it was worse. Even before she insisted on shaving her head, Judith had thin, straight hair, and Miriam's dark curls were the envy of their village. Her brothers also had curly hair, and Judith always felt the lack of it when she was beside them. Because many of the parishioners that her father visited were elderly, they did not spare her feelings.

"Why, that one is plain," they would say. "Doesn't look a bit like your other little darlings, does she?"

Her father would only give his small smile and talk about how every child is a child of God, but he had always considered his Judith to be particularly special. When her mother was with him, she would give him a look of affection, even going so far as to touch his hand, which rankled. Judith hated being a charity case in her own family simply because she was not born with the charms that graced every other sibling. At times, her mother told her that her face was handsome and striking, only she could never think of it that way herself.

But now, she had a different task. She needed to gather information with her father, and she would not be left behind.

The first family that he was visiting was a loud one. On other visits, Judith would have made her excuses as soon as she decently could. She could not understand why some families, even when their children were older, insisted on a level of noise and chaos that made her feel ill straightaway. Though her own brothers could be rambunctious, the children of the Barnes household made the little St Clairs look like angels. The Barnes children were yelling and fighting as much as they could in the little sitting room, and Judith wondered if they were even worse when they had no visitors.

One of the boys seemed eager to show her a younger child, who had just begun to toddle about. "She's my niece," he said. "My niece!"

"She's just lovely," said Judith with a tight smile, edging her chair closer to the hearth, where her father sat with the mother of the babe and an older woman who looked to be that lady's mother. Indeed, she was soon introduced as Mrs Maxwell, and it was clear that she was lady of the house more than her daughter, a timid young lady named Mrs Prudence Barnes.

"You needn't spend your time with the likes of us, you being a rector, Mr St Clair," said the older woman, earning herself a "hush" from her daughter.

"It is a great honour that you have welcomed me into your home," said her father. "And if it would please you, perhaps we might pray. I can also ask my daughter to read. She is a very fine reader."

Judith, who did not mind reading, hoped that they would oblige him. She did not know how many more minutes of listening to the children yell she could manage to endure. Two of them had got into their mother's work basket, and there were now small quantities of thread in many colours scattered all around it. Judith was impressed by the quality of the embroidery itself, with its small and delicate flower motif, and wondered whether the family sold such fine handker-chiefs or only made them for friends. Her parents had spent a great deal of money over the years paying their parishioners for goods and services that they could ill afford. But this year, Judith had a little money to spend on gifts, and she had not bought a thing.

"It's them up at the hall as needs prayers," the older woman said, following Judith's gaze. "They can afford what they like, but that doesn't make them better than anyone. The wages of sin, mark my words."

"Mama," said her daughter, sharper now. "You needn't. We can show some respect."

"That Mr Ramsbury, he didn't show respect, did he?" Mrs Maxwell said. "My own granddaughter had to leave the village."

Judith's father managed to look sympathetic without letting on that he knew nothing of the story. He was too polite to pry, and he was also well aware of what it meant when a young lady "had to leave the village" suddenly.

Mrs Barnes, who must have been at least forty to have both grown children and little ones, lowered her voice. "It wasn't as bad as it might have been, see. She did not have to leave. But there's not a future for her here after what Mr Ramsbury did."

Judith cursed her father. He was still saying nothing, and now she was not going to learn anything.

"Mr Ramsbury," she said. How inconvenient that there were two of them! Mr Theo or Mr Ephraim Ramsbury seemed the likeliest candidates, as they were both elder sons who ought to be addressed that way. But it could even have been Mr Morgan Ramsbury that they were speaking of, or the elderly Mr Horace Ramsbury, bringing the number of possibilities up to four at least. Judith would have to pretend to be very ignorant if she wished to avoid the impropriety of asking outright. "I have not had many occasions to speak with him, but his daughters are charming."

The old woman gave her a sharp look, and she wondered whether she had truly managed to ask a question without asking. There was little that escaped Mrs Maxwell.

"Weren't that Mr Ramsbury. The other one, without children, that Theo Ramsbury. Well, without children that he claims."

"Mama, I must beg you!"

"I can speak plainly, girl. It'll be nothing our guests haven't seen before and nothing they won't see again."

Judith's father, to his credit, did not blush.

He did, however, insist on changing the subject and eventually pressed Judith into reading.

Clearing her throat, she began.

"And Joseph also went up from Galilee, out of the city of Nazareth, into Judaea, unto the city of David, which is called Bethlehem; (because he was of the house and lineage of David:) To be taxed with Mary his espoused wife, being great with child."

It was, indeed, another story of a young woman bearing a child who was not her husband's. But because it was a sacred story, nobody thought to blush.

They left the Barnes family and Mrs Maxwell after Judith had taken her chance to admire all the fine needlework.

She hoped that they had not offended the family with all of the talk about birth, and the virgin birth at that. She herself found that particular part of the Christmas story rather less than creditable, though she never intended to tell her father that.

If she had understood Mrs Barnes correctly, the girl who had to leave the village might not have been with child. Judith hoped that meant she could make a new start somewhere far away, where her reputation would not travel. In that way, she would have an easier time than Louisa-Margaretta Haddington. A well-made gown, no matter how fine, would not be able to hide the evidence of a coming child forever.

It was the next house before she was able to get more information on Mr Morgan Ramsbury. This time, she made sure to use his full name. Perhaps it was not fully correct, but she wanted to make sure she was not gathering information on the widower. And she did not need to hear any more gossip to convince her that Mr Theo Ramsbury was not a gentleman to be trusted.

"Mr Morgan Ramsbury has been so kind to our family," she said after the talk turned (inevitably) to the murder. They were visiting a Miss Finch and her niece, and Judith found it fascinating that both women seemed to have suspicions about the death. Though they voiced them politely ("And her so full of health, too, and so happy"), she could tell that there was a sort of lingering disquiet. And they should not have known that Miss Ross was happy and healthy, as she was in the area for almost no time at all before her death. People must have been talking.

It made her wonder what other rumors were flying about in the village of Brackenfield and how on earth she was to go about discovering them without the friendships and long years of history that would have helped her in her old home.

"Mr Morgan Ramsbury, you say?" said the younger one, Miss Tabitha Finch, and Judith fancied her cheeks were turning a little bit pink. "I'm sure I heard that he had a debt of honour in the next village. It happened just after the family moved in, it did. There was talk of duelling!"

Her aunt quickly shook her head. "My, my. My dear, you do hear the funniest things sometimes. I am sure that we heard something else entirely, and you have it all in a muddle. It was the brother, Mr Theo Ramsbury, with the debt of honour."

The elder Miss Finch, with a look at Judith's father, quickly corrected herself. "That is, we hear that Mr Theo Ramsbury had a debt of honour. It's all talk, I am certain. After all, people will talk when there are newcomers."

Judith had sympathy for the older Miss Finch. She wondered how scared she was of the family. The Haddingtons, as owners of the estate and the village, held many livelihoods in their power. She knew that if she herself were seen as gossiping about family secrets, her father might well be one of the casualties of their wrath. She tried to speak in general terms.

"I am sure that gambling does our nation a great harm," she said. "And yet it is a common pastime for young men nowadays. I confess I do not understand it. I find cards great fun, and all is ruined for me when there are any stakes at all."

Miss Finch, relieved, seized upon her statement. "Well! Miss St Clair. I am sure your father will not mind terribly if we play a little game ourselves, then? Not for any sort of stakes, mind you. Just a little amusement."

And they passed a very pleasant half hour playing Loo while teaching Judith's father the rules all the while. The rules had to be adapted, of course, since they did not have five players, but that made the game even more amusing. Judith herself found that she did not fully remember and was surprised when she and Miss Tabitha Finch formed a better team than she might have expected.

Judith's father smiled more and more as the game went on, and both St Clairs ended up being rather surprised how enjoyable they found the simple parlour amusement. He had never truly approved of cards, but Judith was astonished by his memory. He seemed to never forget a sequence and had all of the ladies around him either laughing or frowning in frustration. By the time they left, Judith had forgotten all about the murders, and her good spirits lasted for most of their walk.

They were interrupted by a man Judith hardly recognized at first. "I am sorry to trouble you, Mr St Clair, Miss St Clair," he said, nearly out of breath. "But I found this cross in the mud, and as I could see both of you in the distance, I thought I should return it."

Judith was surprised that Mr Morgan Ramsbury was

speaking to them and even more surprised that he had noticed the small cross she usually wore. "I am so sorry," she said, holding out her hand. "It is mine."

He placed it in her hand delicately, without touching her skin, and she hid her hands in her muff again.

Judith was unable to speak at first, feeling as she did that losing the cross was some punishment for pretending to "lose" the mourning brooch. After all, the cross had once belonged to her mother.

Her companion also seemed unlikely to speak, but Judith's father was perfectly at ease.

"Thank you," he said. "How are you this morning? How is the family?"

Mr Morgan Ramsbury bobbed his head gently. "We are all well, thank you, sir. We grieve for Miss Ross, but everyone has been very kind."

Judith's mind immediately flew to the source of the kindness, as she imagined many neighbours only wanted to visit for a round of gossip. But she dared not say it.

"What do you remember of your aunt?" she asked rather suddenly. All she knew thus far of Miss Ross was that the lady was rather funny and irreverent.

"She was not my aunt, exactly," said the young man, who was now walking beside Judith as her father strode ahead with rather surprising vigour. "In fact, I feel as if I hardly knew her."

"She would not have said the same of you, surely."

He gave a nervous chuckle. "No, I suppose not. With my mother gone, she seemed to feel that she had some standing to advise me, at least in certain matters."

Judith was reminded of Aunt Leah. "My aunt is much the same."

He nodded. "I should not have been offended, and I do not wish to speak ill of the dead."

There was a pause as Judith waited for Mr Morgan Ramsbury to follow this with a little burst of ill will toward the deceased. But instead, he only cleared his throat.

"Spiritual matters are rather complicated, as I am sure you know, Miss St Clair," he said. "I wish you and your father an excellent morning."

Judith started. They had already reached the rectory, and Papa seemed to have gone in without even bidding farewell to their walking companion. It was uncommonly rude, but then, in the chaos of Miss Ross's death, perhaps one could be permitted such a lapse in manners.

"Good day, Mr Ramsbury," she said.

He nodded, still looking concerned but not unburdening himself of any other memories of his aunt. "Good day, Miss St Clair."

❧ 18 ❧

When Judith and her father came in from their morning of visiting, he was determined to go straight to his study to write letters. At times, he would spend a whole day visiting and come home quite exhausted. Judith was sure that he should simply hire a curate to do most of the work, an opinion shared by Miriam and Aunt Leah, but he wouldn't hear of it.

"I gained this living from my reputation, my dear," he said mildly. "And part of that was that I always tended to every-thing myself. Nothing too small, you know! If I were one of those lazy fellows who hired out all my duties to a simple curate, it would mean that I had accepted the living under false pretences."

Aunt Leah scolded him for his speech, touching his cold hands and shaking her head. "You were a young curate your-self," she said. "Overworked and underpaid, without enough hours for your family. But, my dear brother, 'curate' need not mean 'man of all work' if you do not wish it. You could treat your own curate much better."

But he retired to his study. To write letters and, Judith was certain, to sleep uninterrupted.

This left Judith free, and she knew that she needed to make a call.

"Aunt Leah," she called, walking about the hall as if she were engaged in a genuine search. "Have you seen my mourning brooch?"

"No," the reply came from the sitting room. "But I am sure you shall find it."

"I will check with Miriam and my brothers," she called back then made a show of going around the house, asking each person she saw. As she expected, nobody could say they had seen it since the recent visit to the Haddingtons' house. She went back to her aunt, who was sitting and writing letters of her own while the boys ran about, playing some sort of game that involved a good deal of whispered laughter. Judith reflected that at least they were a bit quieter indoors than the Barnes family, though when loose out of doors, they were certainly just as rambunctious. Or perhaps, after the years of caring for them, she was simply inured to their special variety of chaos.

For a moment, Judith reflected that she rarely spoke to her brothers. She had once enjoyed their games, but with Mama gone, she had become as strict and unsmiling as any governess. Aunt Leah gave them a great deal more attention, and they seemed to be making the most of it.

Her aunt was now untangling wool from a knitting doll and scolding Aaron and Moses for keeping Joseph from learning how to use it.

"Moses, you wish to be a soldier," she was saying, her hands unknotting the wool that Joseph had managed to get into a horrible mess. "How are you to manage if you cannot do any of your own mending?"

"I shall ask Judith to do it," he said. "Or Miriam."

"But would they be with you if you were in the army?"

Judith noticed that Aunt Leah seemed quite well. She was crouched near the fire with her nephews with not the slightest complaint of the leg she had once claimed she could not walk on.

Judith cleared her throat. "Aunt Leah, I cannot find my mourning brooch, and it must be somewhere. I did not have it this morning, but I had it yesterday."

Aunt Leah put the doll down slowly.

"You did not think to put it on before you made your calls?" she asked, eyebrows raised. "That is not like you."

Judith flushed. "Well, I suppose I am distracted. We all are, with the, well, the trouble the day before last and then so many calls to make today."

"It was kind of you to accompany your father."

Her aunt's customary inquisitiveness and bright tone were both lacking, and Judith found her cheeks growing pink as she stood before her. "Well. I suppose I had better go to Wycliff Castle to look for it."

"Yes, I suppose you better had."

There was a pause, but before Judith took her leave, Aunt Leah stood and touched her arm. In a voice too low for the children to hear, she said, "Be careful."

Moses and Aaron were now tussling over the knitting doll, having decided it was for boys after all, and poor Joseph had little hope of seeing the thing again. But Aunt Leah kept her gaze fixed on Judith.

Judith did not draw her arm away. She was too shocked. "Careful? Of what?"

"I believe I can speak freely. We are alone, or as near as."

Both looked at the young boys, who were now playing at being soldiers cooking a meal around the fire. They were so absorbed in their game they could not have heard more than a word of what was said between the ladies. In spite of their papa's best efforts, they did love the romance of fighting the beast Napoleon. Papa might continue to forbid them from acquiring lead soldiers, but their games tended to battles and army life all the same.

"Be careful of becoming too close to Miss Haddington," said Aunt Leah. "She is rich, to be sure, but her position is a precarious one."

Judith felt an unaccustomed surge of friendship towards Miss Haddington the moment she was warned away from the acquaintance. She responded with equal coldness.

"I am to suppose that Miss Haddington herself is the best judge of her own position."

Her aunt did not smile. "As you like. But Judith, remember that I know more of the world than you do. You would do well to listen."

❧ 19 ❧

Judith did listen. In fact, that was her curse.

Miss Leah St Clair, had she the privilege of listening to her niece's thoughts, would have heard a young person at war with herself.

As she walked to Wycliff Castle, Judith attempted to convince herself that her aunt could not know a great deal about a young lady she had yet to meet. And yet she could not pretend to be fully ignorant of the circumstances. A young woman who wished to make a hasty marriage, especially one that would give her child a name, was in a precarious position, no matter how rich. Judith wondered that the family had not tried to go further afield. If they had fled to the continent, perhaps, they could have gone to a quiet little hamlet under assumed names and all come back without a murmur, sending the child to be raised in some distant location.

There was no rain, but fog had come rolling in from the mountains. Judith wished it were limited to the morning, but it seemed to come and go at all hours. She stayed on the road so she would not get lost. She cursed the wild country.

Perhaps it was Napoleon that convinced Mrs Haddington that she needed to marry her daughter off and have done with it. Nowhere on the continent was safe, as nobody knew where the evil man might next attack. Indeed, Judith had begun to feel that even England was not safe, though she knew enough not to voice those thoughts while her brothers were listening. In a world where nations could topple and her mother could die, there was little that was certain.

This brought her back to her aunt's words as she came closer to the house. Even through the fog, though she could not see it, she could sense its presence, and she wondered if there was anything improper in her friendship with Miss Haddington.

She decided that there was not. Miss Haddington, after all, was not a friend. If there were strange moments of understanding between them, they were overshadowed by Miss Haddington's fine clothes and brusque manners. And now that she had enough to identify the brutal man who had killed Miss Ross, all she needed to do was present it to her unfortunate library companion. Louisa-Margaretta would be disappointed to learn that her cousin was not only a rogue but a violent one at that, but it was Judith's duty to tell the truth. After that, apart from the village fete and church on Sundays, they did not need to have anything to do with one another.

In the fog, she nearly walked into the side of the grand house. She could hear a conversation from the room above. It would have been madness to open a window to the damp, yet it seemed to her that this must have happened. She could smell air rich with smoke, and she heard the voices of gentlemen.

"I must have a moment for a conference with you," came a voice she vaguely recognized. It was the older Mr Ramsbury, she realized, Mr Horace Ramsbury. And he was speaking with his nephew, Mr Ephraim Ramsbury.

"I must see to my daughters," answered the younger gentleman. "I cannot entrust their education to others. And Agnes was quite upset about the hunt."

"Strange thing, Agnes being so upset. She must have seen dozens of them."

"Yes, and each time, she cries more and more. It does not suit her, and I must say that I am surprised it is being considered for a house in mourning. A hunt is frivolous at the best of times and highly improper now."

There was a pause, then Mr Horace Ramsbury answered. "Apparently, Miss Haddington insisted."

There was a short bark of laughter from the younger gentleman and a reluctant chuckle from the older one, who continued, "Are you quite sure you wouldn't like to see more of her? She's beautiful, and she's your cousin. And you should be rescuing her from a very unfortunate decision."

"I'm not sure she wants rescuing, Uncle. She's made it amply clear to me that she considers herself a spinster."

"Stuff and nonsense. She will change her mind. Women always do. But as it happens, it was marriage I wanted to speak with you about."

"I do not intend to marry again."

"Wait! Not your marriage. Another matter entirely. Please."

"I must beg you to excuse me."

There was the sound of the door closing, and Judith heard a sigh and a soliloquy. "Not your marriage at all. A marriage that I made long ago, when I was younger and even more foolish."

Judith waited, willing herself not to sneeze from either the fog or the odour of pipe smoke, which had always sickened her. Because her father was an abstemious man, she never had to worry about the cloying smoke at home.

She was still standing there when she heard two young men speaking. Gardeners, perhaps. It wouldn't do if they discovered her skulking by the house.

She found her way to the steps and knocked on the front door, though entering Wycliff Castle still seemed strange to her. It was as if, instead of relieving her from the cold fog, the place was swallowing her whole.

❧ 20 ❧

Louisa-Margaretta was walking down the stairs when Miss St Clair was announced. The poor thing was soaked nearly to the bone, and all from such a short, easy walk. Her thin hair fairly clung to her skull, and she was shivering.

Louisa-Margaretta drew her guest to the music room, asking for tea from a maid as she passed by.

Only when the door was closed did she begin to speak.

"I'm glad you've come," she said. "But I did not send for you. I was going to claim that I had just found your mourning brooch so I would have a reason to walk over to the rectory. How did you know that I had news?"

"You have news?" Miss St Clair said. "Well, I suppose it was time. I have news as well."

The door opened, and the tea was brought in. Louisa-Margaretta was mother. She did it well, pouring the perfect amount of hot tea without flinching and making elegant little remarks as she did so. Only when a decent amount of time had passed, in which she gave fulsome compliments on Miss

St Clair's "exceedingly lovely gown," did she go back to the door and close it gently.

"Thank you for bringing this matter to my attention, Miss St Clair," she said. "And now, we can lay it to rest."

Miss St Clair paused. She had taken a sip of tea and pronounced it "very refreshing," although the grimace that she did not quite manage to hide had made it clear that she found the elixir lacking. Perhaps she took an unseemly amount of milk and sugar with her tea at home, a vice which no lady could ever admit in company. She set the cup on its saucer and stared.

"Tell me," she said. "How are we going to lay it to rest?"

Louisa-Margaretta sat with a straight back, every inch the grand lady who has invited a poor villager into her stately home. "You said that it was one of the family," she stated. "I did not believe you. But that was before I saw the way my cousin, Mr Morgan Ramsbury, had been behaving."

"Mr Morgan Ramsbury?" said Miss St Clair. "What, the man who never talks?"

"There is a reason that he never talks," said Louisa-Margaretta. "It is his guilty conscience."

"But what reason would he have to kill your aunt?" said Miss St Clair, her voice rising for the first time since the beginning of her visit.

"I cannot give a reason," said Louisa-Margaretta primly. "But I suppose it was there for me to see all along. You see, even the Bible talks about murder for the sake of love and money. I must assume that my cousin's motivations were something along those lines."

Miss St Clair stood, went to the window, then came back. Her hands were in fists at her sides, and she looked as if she might smash the teacup or cry or both. "You have no right to make an unjust accusation of that sort," she sputtered. "I cannot imagine that Mr Morgan Ramsbury inherits anyway. By rights, it would be his elder brother."

"Everyone inherits," said Louisa-Margaretta. She may have known little about money, but she knew that the son and heir was rarely the end of the story. And in the case of her Aunt Matilda, the money would most likely be divided amongst relatives somehow. She knew that her aunt lived largely on the generous nature of others. Louisa-Margaretta's own father had grumbled, at times, about the difficulty of supporting such a proud woman. She never would take the funds that she needed outright or admit that she was suffering for the lack of them. Louisa-Margaretta's mother was more patient, disguising her support as elegant little gifts and invitations to stay for ever-longer visits. Still, Aunt Matilda must have some little money, and perhaps she had left what she could to Mr Morgan Ramsbury.

"If you believed this, you would have to tell your family."

"I shall tell my mama," said Louisa-Margaretta, taking a lazy sip of tea. Once she had divined that the murderer was her taciturn cousin, she had been far less afraid. Aunt Matilda had been making vague remarks about Cousin Morgan the whole visit, though Louisa-Margaretta had not been interested enough to divine her purpose. She thought it was something to do with religion, and she got quite enough spiritual lectures from Mama. The man was not likely to do anything rash, after all, and she would not need to tell everyone. He might keep lurking in rooms where he did not belong, walking at odd hours, avoiding the family, but Louisa-Margaretta did not think that he would kill again. "Mama is practical. She can solve this."

Miss St Clair had become so agitated that her voice rose to a pitch Louisa-Margaretta had never heard. "What, by poisoning him? Or sending him off to war?"

"He needn't go to war," Louisa-Margaretta said. She herself had never needed to soothe children, and she did not think she was making a very good job of it with her ever-more-angry guest. Miss St Clair resembled a little boy who had not got his share of pudding, and surely, she needed a firm but loving elder to set her to rights. "He can simply leave before Christmas. Now that he's got the poisoning over with, I'm sure he won't do it again."

"And you're not angry that this cousin killed your aunt for money, and for very little money?"

Louisa-Margaretta sighed. She didn't know how to explain that she and her aunt had never got on and that the love that Aunt Matilda had once bestowed on all around her had gone missing years ago. For though Louisa-Margaretta had to listen to her father's comments about having a houseguest who demanded the finest meat and drank an unseemly amount of wine, she had heard worse things from her aunt's mouth for many years. Aunt Matilda spared nobody, and her barbs found their mark much of the time. Oddly, many of them seemed centred around Louisa-Margaretta's figure and marriage prospects, as if making a young woman feel cross would somehow goad her into the grand contentment of matrimony.

Indeed, sometimes, the insults were worse, and sometimes, it was the compliments. Before, when Louisa-Margaretta was younger, it had always been things such as, "My dear niece, I am sure all the other girls wish they had your figure." A compliment that was an insult against most of their sex and therefore rather unsettling.

More recently, since Louisa-Margaretta had gained both a size and a level of strength that did not appeal to her aunt, it had been insults about such a "promising young woman" wasting the advantages she had been given. Louisa-

Margaretta had been presented at court, she had a famously large dowry, and she'd had so many dancing lessons that even when she lost her concentration, her movements remained both precise and elegant.

Louisa-Margaretta picked at a thread on the bombazine of her black skirts. She knew that she ought to mourn her aunt, but she could not seem to summon the proper feelings. She ought to be wailing and gnashing her teeth, while privately, she was not surprised that her poor cousin had been driven mad. Indeed, her mother seemed to be the only person with kind words for Aunt Matilda at the end.

"Thank you for your help," she found herself saying. "But this truly is to be a family affair. I do not think my cousin has learned anything of that night, and he need never know that we were in the library."

"He does not need to know it because he is not a killer," said Miss St Clair. "His brother, Theo Ramsbury, is."

At this, Louisa-Margaretta laughed aloud, then poured herself some more tea. "His brother," she said, "is a very gay man. But it is all show. He is quite harmless."

Miss St Clair flushed, but she was on safer ground now. The tears that had threatened to spill earlier were gone.

"He is a seducer," she said. "And he has a debt of honour in the next village. Duelling is involved somehow." She lowered her voice as she said the last part.

Louisa-Margaretta shook her head. Miss St Clair liked to portray herself as a worldly young woman, and yet the man she described could have been nearly anyone in Louisa-Margaretta's social circle. In the haut ton, behaviour such as her cousin's was common, even expected. He was young and unmarried.

"The seduction and the debt of honour," she said, "are part of who my cousin is." She held up a hand at Miss St Clair's objections. "I cannot defend them, and as you shall note, I have not listened to Mama's request that I marry him. I should hate for him to make me look a fool. And I think that men look ever so silly when they talk of duelling. But it hardly amounts to murder."

"It amounts to a very good reason to kill your aunt," said Miss St Clair. "And as the first son, he would stand to inherit more, would he not?"

"Only from his father," Louisa-Margaretta said firmly. "And as to this debt of honour, I am sure that his father would be able to pay it. So you see, there would be no trouble there, either. When did he acquire it, do you know?"

"About a month ago, just after the family arrived," said Miss St Clair, looking smug for the first time at her superior information. "It was in the next village."

Louisa-Margaretta sighed with relief and added tea to her guest's cup, though Miss St Clair had yet to take a second sip. "He only arrived a week ago," she said. "Less than a week. He came from the continent."

And she thought, for a moment, about her cousin's travels. He lived for these journeys to the continent. It was one reason he claimed he could never marry.

Indeed, even with the spectre of Napoleon, the trip had sounded absolutely lovely. "Having seen Paris a dozen times, I may seek other cities," he claimed and gave no more thought to that ruler. He had spent months in the countryside near Naples, claiming it was the most beautiful he could remember anywhere, sunny and warm with exceedingly charming locals and travel companions.

Louisa-Margaretta frowned a bit as she thought of it. Surely, his voyage had been costly. He was a gentleman, but he stood to inherit from his father, and while he did not have access to that capital, he should not have been spending a very great deal. The Ramsbury family was an old one, to be sure, but they were not uniformly rich. But Cousin Theo always wanted travel and his own accommodations and very good food besides. Her own father had grumbled at this ostentatious idleness, but Cousin Theo laughed off any talk of finding a profession.

"Well," she said. "It appears that we do not agree. But at any rate, we may as well make the best of things."

Miss St Clair frowned. "If you acknowledge that my theory may be correct, quite apart from the debt of honour, why would you not act to protect your own family?"

Louisa-Margaretta thought for a moment. She was certain that she was right — that it was her milder cousin, Morgan the lamb, who had surely stepped outside his typically diffident nature to poison the cake. But if it had been his brother instead, a seducer to whom lies were as natural as breathing, might there not be more danger there?

It was all theoretical to her. She felt in no more danger than she had ever been. What was more, she felt like an idiot for having thought it all so serious. Perhaps it was not even murder at all.

"You don't think my aunt wished to die," she said, an unaccustomed hesitation in her voice. "But she could have asked someone else to poison her if she did wish to take her own life. Sometimes, cowards cannot manage without help."

Miss St Clair was openly staring. She went over to the fire and stood gazing into it, her back to Louisa-Margaretta for several minutes. When she finally spoke, it was with a strained note of martyrdom.

"Everyone has said that she was healthy and that she seemed happy, even. Perhaps giddy with happiness. Why would she wish to poison herself or seek help in dying? It cannot be. She was only in the country to celebrate Christmas with her family."

Louisa-Margaretta looked around the lavishly decorated room. Their new home, even if it was a prison to her, should not have been a dangerous place. Her aunt, who drank, swore, and always spoke out of turn, had doubtless made an enemy of someone in the family.

She reflected that it was probably not uncommon. Because her Aunt Matilda was hardly part of the family. Having come up in very hard circumstances, she had lost all of her family, ending with her sister. She had no profession, no fortune, only the gifts she had received in the years since her sister had married exceedingly well.

"She was not truly with family. She did not even share a surname with us."

"But her sister did," countered Miss St Clair, somehow managing to make it sound as if Louisa-Margaretta had said something vulgar.

"Pardon?"

"Miss Ross was the sister of Mrs Sally Ramsbury, the adopted mother of Mr Ephraim Ramsbury. That means that in some sense, she was very close to the family, even if she was not a blood relation."

Louisa-Margaretta shook her head. She was clearly getting dizzy after so much talk of plots and murder. And all of the fuss over it had kept her from achieving any of her aims. She had not been able to talk any sense into her mother. She had intended to use the Christmas season to beg both Mama's forgiveness and her permission for an unusual match. Failing that, at least to get word to Isaac, which ought to have been her chief aim every morning.

Their first meeting flashed before her again. It had been in the British Museum, as were most of the meetings after. That is, before they reached an understanding and started truly meeting in secret.

The thought of it made her flush. The upper floor, where the modern paintings were displayed, seemed the only place in London where she could be free of both a chaperone and the judgement that came along with such a party. It could be her Aunt Matilda or the timid Mrs Kitt, whom her mother kept on as a companion for her far past the year when Louisa-Margaretta was expected to have married.

Her favourite picture was one of a ship on the ocean. Though she loved paintings of romance and of heroes who were depicted in both detail and clothing that would never have been allowed in any other context. But the ocean painting obliterated all those. She loved the waves, the sense of disappearing into a landscape and the promise of distant shores.

That was what she had seen when he first spoke with her. He had manners, and he knew that they should not speak without an introduction.

So she created one.

She dropped her handkerchief slowly, lazily, letting it flutter from her gloved fingers to her feet as she stared at the painting. She hoped that no well-meaning child or granny would come and pick it up, and indeed, he was the first to do so.

"Miss, if you'll excuse me. You've dropped your hand-kerchief."

"Pardon?" she said, meeting his eyes. She knew that she could have picked it up herself, just after he spoke to her, but to do so would have been to cut the conversation short.

"Your handkerchief," he said, bending over to retrieve it.

"Thank you so much," she said. "I'm sorry, I have forgotten your name."

She saw him start. "I'm sorry, have we been introduced?"

"Yes, of course! It was . . . at some assembly, I cannot remember. I have been to so many this season. When one is in town, they all run together, or at least I find it to be so."

He looked confused, and she guessed his thoughts. The

poor gentleman must have been wondering how he could have forgotten her when he was clearly taken with her now.

And she with him. She had seen him passing through, admiring paintings, and for the first time, a conversation with a handsome man did not leave her feeling betrayed or stupid. Rather, it left her with a sense that at last, there was one time when her heart did not completely lead her astray. Here was a man of sense and breeding, but more importantly, a man she could not resist.

"I'm terribly sorry," she said. "I'm no good when it comes to remembering names."

She saw a flash of hesitation, and she admired him for it. If he said that she was mistaken, that they had never met, then they would lose the chance of meeting now. And she knew that he very much wished to speak to her.

"Mr Isaac Rodrigo," he said. "A pleasure to see you once again, Miss?"

"Miss Haddington," she said, smiling at his accurate assumption that she was not married. At her age, more and more strangers had been taking her for a married lady, and when they found she was still unmarried, they either pressed her for a reason or made hopeful pronouncements about the happy matrimony that ought to be nearing.

"I hope you are enjoying the season?" she said politely. If she were to maintain the pretence of some acquaintance, she must be sure not to give herself away by expressing anything too specific.

"I am," he managed. "Though as you surmised, the assemblies can be rather taxing. Are you enjoying yourself?"

"I am enjoying my time in town," she said. "I love the amusements and the art, though I confess that if I ever attend another assembly, I shall die of either hunger or boredom. The refreshments at Almack's are even more sparing than I remember, and my appetite is most unladylike."

At this, he laughed heartily for the first time. "I am glad to hear it. I find bird-like appetites very strange indeed. And with five sisters, I believe I can say with some authority that the public perception of women as beings who seldom need refreshment is a most scandalous falsehood."

"There is nothing I like better," she said, "than a cup of tea with some decent sandwiches. Hearty ones that stick to the bones."

The memory of what she had said reminded her of the present. She was not in Isaac's company but seated next to the stubborn Miss St Clair. A very sorry plate of delicate sandwiches had been brought in next to the tea, and she grabbed one with some haste. She was hungry and suddenly quite exhausted.

That was exactly what nobody had told her about imprisonment — how very tiring it could be. Her mother had carefully prepared her location. None of the servants could be trusted to get word to even a seemingly innocuous go-between such as Mrs Kitt, and her mother had seen to it that she would not be able to post a letter in the village, either. She needed to find someone who would help her.

"Do you write many letters, Miss St Clair?" she asked.

The girl frowned. Louisa-Margaretta should have forced a sandwich on her. Really, Miss St Clair must have eaten almost nothing, and she was quite pale.

"I do correspond with my old friends. Or one of them, at least. But I confess I have not written to her in weeks."

"Well," said Louisa-Margaretta, clearing her throat. "I need to get a message to someone in town. Perhaps you could include a sheet from me in one of your letters."

This was met only with a frown. "It might be faster if you sent it direct. I'm not sure how long it would take my friend Letty to deliver a message. Does it concern your aunt?"

Louisa-Margaretta thought hastily. She would never be

able to explain everything in just one letter, not if the message was going to be read by others. She had so much to say to Isaac, chiefly that she still loved him and wished to marry, but also details of her strange days in Wycliff Castle. She could have pretended that she was shaken by Aunt Matilda's death and wished to inform a friend, but she had not been clever enough to invent such a story.

Also, the young woman currently sitting with a stiff back on the luxurious new pink chair was the daughter of a rector and seemed to have a very religious view of propriety. She could not be trusted not to turn with Louisa-Margaretta's secret. After all, she had been talking of nothing but punishment and justice since she arrived.

"Pay me no mind," Louisa-Margaretta said, trying to force a laugh as she wandered over to one of the small tables. "Here is your brooch. I thought you might be missing it."

Miss St Clair took the brooch with a murmur of thanks, and Louisa-Margaretta sighed. She could not truly trust this person, and if she went on too long about letters, Miss St Clair might well ask why she did not write to her correspondent directly. "I will not burden you with my little missive at the moment. I suppose I am only trying to think of a subject that is not grim."

"You needn't dwell on the subject of murder," said Miss St Clair, gathering her skirts as if she were about to take her leave while remaining seated. "But I think we must tell someone, at least, even if we do not yet agree on all the facts."

Louisa-Margaretta waved it away. "Whom could we possibly tell? Nobody would believe us. We would get a scolding for hiding in the library during a ball, and that would be that."

Miss St Clair bit her lip as she stood. "I cannot help feeling that I am leaving you in grave danger for a second time. I will search for more proofs against your cousin, but I am not sure that I shall find anything."

Louisa-Margaretta shook her head. "You may rest easy, Miss St Clair. I do not sense danger in this house."

What she did not care to add was that she would not be within the walls of the house a great deal in the coming weeks. And when she did escape its walls, she would be far less protected.

$\mathscr{H}$ 21 $\mathscr{H}$

Louisa-Margaretta loved riding to hounds. She felt as if it were in her blood, though many of her companions thought it was nearly scandalous for a lady to ride. Her own mother had come close to not allowing it, but the first year, Louisa-Margaretta insisted that she would race her older brother Loftus with the hunt itself as a prize. And she would do so on a horse, if you please, not a pony. Mrs Haddington was not fond of gambling, either, but when she saw her daughter best a boy four years older, she could not keep herself from admitting that it would be unjust to deprive the hunt itself of Louisa-Margaretta.

For some time, they had compromised. Louisa-Margaretta always rode at home, but her mother could deny her permission if they were at the home of a particularly stuffy family who would not like a lady riding. On these occasions, Louisa-Margaretta was not forced to attend the hunt and pretend to enjoy the picnics and other unsatisfactory amusements designated for the ladies, but she did not ride, either.

With the family in mourning, the hunt they had planned was not going to come off, so Louisa-Margaretta convinced her father to plan a small shooting party instead. It was to be only the family and their guests, so in spite of their situation, it was not improper. They invited the rector, but to her great relief, he declined. He did not hunt, and nobody from his family would be attending. Haughty Miss St Clair could keep her accusations to herself.

When Mr St Clair joined the party in the morning, she winced. The poor man should better have stayed home, and Louisa-Margaretta had to wonder at his sudden change of heart. He looked as if he did not know how to hold a gun, much less handle one. Refusing the invitation was surely the wiser choice for such a sorry hunter. Mr Bragg hardly looked better. The man had bloodshot eyes, even though their start had not been particularly early, and he kept saying "Hmm" as he surveyed the territory. He had terrible knees, and every time he had to walk downhill for even a yard, he staggered about with his walking stick like a much older man.

Louisa-Margaretta's papa was a terrible shot. He liked strutting about during the party, smelling the gunpowder and feeling very fine indeed in his special clothes, but he rarely managed to hit a bird. When he did hit one, Louisa-Margaretta knew that it was often due to her secretly allowing him to claim one of her birds as his own. She suspected that other hunting partners did this as well. Her papa was not vain, but it would be tedious for him if he never hit anything at all.

Cousin Theo attended the shooting party with his younger brother, Morgan, and both appeared to shoot about as well as dear Papa. He got a few shots off, but he was terribly inconsistent, and his brother was so nervous that Louisa-Margaretta doubted he had hit a single bird.

Cousin Ephraim also came, under duress, after Mrs Haddington promised to look after his girls for the day. Louisa-Margaretta heard her speaking under her breath about finding a proper governess, but she knew that her mother would be a devoted aunt. Little Anna and Agnes might find their religious studies strange, but their morning would not be dull.

Cousin Ephraim was by far the best shot of the men, second only to Louisa-Margaretta in the shooting party, though he had little to contribute by way of conversation. And he did not seem to be enjoying shooting the birds down, sighing every few minutes and looking about as if he, too, were planning an escape.

Louisa-Margaretta, now genuinely curious, asked him how he learned to shoot.

"My father liked it," he said simply. "It was one of the things he liked to do, so I used to go along for his company. Now that he is dead, I never shoot."

"Well, you are shooting today."

"I expect for the same reason that the poor rector is," he said, standing as they prepared to change locations. Louisa-Margaretta would not have minded staying in the field near the house for a bit longer. Perhaps the poor master thought that a spot with a better view of the terrain might improve the performance of the men.

She could have told him his efforts would be fruitless.

"What would that reason be?" Louisa-Margaretta asked Cousin Ephraim, trying to understand why Mr St Clair had come. Before he answered, she saw him roll his eyes when he believed himself unobserved. Really, even for a widower, his manners were rather shocking. When his daughters were near, he was tolerable, but the rest of the time, he hardly seemed to listen to a word she said. She tried to remember if he had been quite so sour the whole time or if he was more affected by their Aunt Matilda's death than he cared to admit. He might have been reminded of the death of his dear wife, which was rather touching. Or perhaps he had treated his aunt with the same disrespect and contempt that he seemed to show all women.

It was not a cheering thought.

"The rector is here because he believes we need comforting," he said. "And he doubtless thought better of refusing an invitation in a family's hour of need."

They looked back. The party was slowly making its way up the peak. His father, Mr Horace Ramsbury, was leading the group as they wound their way through the trees.

"If I had known it would take this long to walk half a mile," he muttered, "I certainly might have reconsidered, even under the circumstances. I doubt they have even remembered to move half the birds."

And he shuffled back down the hill, either to help or complain. Louisa-Margaretta imagined the latter was much more likely.

She made quick work of the hill herself, not stopping once before she reached the top. If Derbyshire had not been her prison, she could have found herself falling in love with the scenery. Riding to hounds would have been beautiful amongst the peaks, she knew, and the frost made her feel awake if not elated. She had some hope when she saw glimpses of the sun.

If only she could share her feelings with Isaac! She brought out the paper and pencil she had carefully concealed. She could not exactly run about hiding an inkwell in her fitted clothing, but she knew that she could write poems on sheaves of paper and hide those. Her feelings were no secret to her family, and anyone in the village who had not heard of her shame would hear of it soon enough. No, it was humiliating that she could not escape, could not share any words of love with the man who most needed to hear them. She would not admit that she had a very great need of his words as well. It was too soon to ask why he had not found her, either with a letter or in person. She must suppose him to be trying, as she was.

She began to write. The rest of the party would reach the top eventually. She knew her time was short.

"The winter's come, but leaves are on the tree

As if bereft of life, they cannot fall

But keep their places, trembling, with the —"

She saw the shot and heard it at the same time.

Then a loud noise made her flinch and tumble to her knees. It was in the cliffside directly above her head, and the rock as it split nearly fell in her face. Stupidly, she had turned to look, because it seemed as if there were some kind of animal above her head, not a bullet.

She could not shriek. She had no voice at all, and at first, she could not move, until she was running, trembling, down the hill, not stopping until she reached the shooting party.

Mr Haddington was a devoted papa, and usually, at the slightest sign of distress, he went immediately to his daughter to placate her. It was a bad habit, and one he had made no attempt to correct. It was also one he repeated with all of his granddaughters. With his grandsons, there was just as much concern in his eyes, but he encouraged them to take their bumps, bruises, and slights "as men." With the ladies of the family, he had no such compunction.

But even he did not notice his daughter, trembling and pale, leaning against a tree to support herself after she had run back down the hill, nearly falling, to where the party was gathered.

"I can't manage! I can't possibly!" said Mr Bragg then let loose with a string of curses that would have amused Louisa-Margaretta had the man not seemed the epitome of madness. "Why, all of you out here, when she is not cold, just shooting! Get a brace, will you! No, I will not have it!"

He was reduced to a fit of sobs, though he was still speaking. She was not surprised to see Cousin Morgan backing away from the fray, picking up the gun Mr Bragg had thrown aside and looking for anything else that might have been dropped.

She was, however, quite surprised to see the rector standing by Mr Bragg, who was all but foaming at the mouth. He certainly displayed every other sign of madness.

The rector was murmuring, and she could not have said whether it was an incantation or a prayer. Her papa called for brandy, but the rector's voice was stern.

"No. Tea, or coffee if we have it. He needs a hot drink, not a strong one."

Louisa-Margaretta doubted that Mr Bragg could hold a cup without flinging it about, but the rector held it for him, blowing on it then touching it to the other man's lips with a gentleness that would not have been out of place in a nanny or a sickroom nurse. She was so fascinated that she had stopped trembling, but this did not keep her from noticing the rest of the party.

Cousin Ephraim was sitting on the ground, staring at his boots as though he could look nowhere else. The more cosmopolitan Cousin Theo was sitting with a pack of cards, shuffling them again and again, looking quite bored.

His father was nowhere to be seen.

22

Judith was still taking inventory in her father's new church. Numbers had always spoken to her, and because nobody was particularly interested in women who studied mathematics, keeping track of money and hymnals was all she found herself fit for. Instead of starting in the vestry, she began her task in the small sanctuary to be sure that she would not miss anything. It was as if the simplest arithmetic, which she had been able to do in her head from four years of age, was the only thing she would ever be permitted to use. She had often complained bitterly to her mother about this.

"Judith, most fathers would not let their daughters see their accounts at all," she had always said. "Papa entrusts you with everything in the family. It is a great honour."

"I would be entrusted with much more were I a man," she said.

"I hardly think being a clerk at a bank would suit you, my dear. Are they not in famously difficult positions, at all hours, for very little pay?"

"I would rather not be a clerk, Mama. I would much prefer to own a bank."

Her mother could not help but laugh.

If Judith did not receive the response she wanted from this, she would make a face. "The Countess of Jersey owns a bank, and she is not the only one."

"Well, my dear, most people do not own banks. Ladies and gentlemen alike are not typically granted that privilege."

Judith knew that simply having enough money for food and parishioners who always helped provide for them should have been blessing enough. But counting the sums of money her family needed, as well as all of the items in the rectory and the church, was not the most taxing use of her gifts. Mathematics as an art form was most satisfying when used for complex problems, not dull housekeeping tasks. Judith hardly knew whether she would prefer the riches of banks and investments or the more academic pursuits of geometry and calculus. Both seemed equally out of reach. With a sigh, she determined that she would go to the vestry to record the sums, even though she was sure she would remember them.

The door was locked, but it had been disturbed. Judith knew that her father had the only key. Mr and Mrs Haddington had been very particular on this point. Both had a very grave fear of theft that was hardly warranted so far in the mountainous countryside, especially since the vestry held only her father's vestments for services and many books of records. Mr Haddington's fear was born of having grown up in a rough part of London, Mrs Haddington's of the knowledge that they had a good many things worth stealing. It was a secret of the very rich, who might talk in laughing tones of the cost of country houses or fine carriages but without forgetting how very few families had even a tiny fraction of what one of their jewels or snuff boxes would fetch.

Judith wondered if a child had disturbed the door. The

outer door seemed untouched, but then her father insisted on leaving the church unlocked at many hours of the day. Giving his parishioners opportunities to come and pray or sit in silence was important to him. He would never be a rector who simply arrived on Sunday and passed his duties on to a curate after he had finished waving his patrons out the door.

She was so focused on her sums that she would have missed a little noise, but there was a great rattling at the vestry door, and Miss Haddington tumbled in. "I must speak with you," she said, shivering.

Judith started. "I'm sorry, we have no refreshments here. But surely you would like a cup of tea? We could go through to the rectory."

"No," said her visitor sharply, going back to the door and peering into the church then nearly slamming the door behind her. "We cannot be overheard."

"Well," said Judith. "All right. But take a blanket, at least. I know my father keeps one in this room. Truly, you do not look at all well."

She found the blanket without too much trouble. Her father was a frugal man, and he did not like to make a fire if he could not help it. But Judith began laying one, as Miss Haddington looked cold. Judith spoke, her back to her guest, as she got a good blaze going.

"Miss Haddington," she said, "whatever has happened to bring you here? Are you not meant to be out shooting with the men?"

"Someone tried to kill me," she said in a quiet voice. "Whoever it was that killed Aunt Matilda, he is vicious. And he must know that we were in the library."

Judith turned around, trying not to betray the pace of her heart. She wanted to know whether she was in danger, but thinking of the shoot, she had only one question. "Where is my father?"

"Oh, with that mad Mr Bragg, I imagine. They must be at the house by now. Your father was the only one who could do anything with him."

"What happened?" said Judith, not convinced by this answer. If Mr Bragg was mad, she needed to get her father away from him.

"Someone tried to shoot me, and they very nearly hit their mark!" cried Miss Haddington. "I ought to be happy that everyone on that shoot could not get a brace of pheasants if they fell from the skies themselves. Otherwise, I might well have died."

She herself slumped down by the fire, and Judith stayed, hoping the flames would stop the cold spreading through her own body.

"I need you to tell me something," she said.

"Anything," said Louisa-Margaretta, suddenly listless. It was as if sharing her story and having it believed had reminded her of her exhaustion.

"I need you to tell me everything that your Aunt Matilda did before she was killed."

$\mathscr{H}$ 23 $\mathscr{H}$

Louisa-Margaretta thought back to her aunt's arrival, trying to tell Judith every detail she could remember. Matilda Ross made a point of never being on time to anything, and their Christmas holiday was the same. She claimed that she would come early on December fifteenth, to join the rest of the party, but they waited on her in vain.

Mr Bragg had come early on the fourteenth then spent most of his time striding about in the grounds or the house. Louisa-Margaretta had begged her mother for the reason for the odd man's presence. Unlike her cousins, eligible bachelors who could give Louisa-Margaretta a tidy and respectable offer, Mr Bragg was married. In fact, he had been married for many years, and his children were grown.

Her mother had some story about how Mr Bragg's wife was going to travel longer to see their second-eldest son, but Mr Bragg had business and could not spare so many days. It was a strange explanation, however, given that he could apparently spare the time and expense of coming all the way to Derbyshire. When Louisa-Margaretta asked how her parents knew him, she was told that he was a "friend of the family" of long standing, even though Louisa-Margaretta could not recall ever having heard his name.

The Ramsbury surname, of course, was shared by most of the party. Cousin Theo, who had arrived the night before, was the other latecomer. He described in great detail his travels on the continent and the lack of romance England held in comparison. It was as if he were determined not to be impressed by Derbyshire. In his telling, he had seen grander peaks nearly every place he had travelled, particularly Switzerland and Austria, and he did not wish to bother with Derbyshire's famous peaks, though "a spot of cards might be just the thing."

Cousin Morgan came with their father, Uncle Horace, a week earlier. He was studying at Oxford, and it was his father's greatest wish that he might become a man of the cloth. He blushed whenever this idea was raised, and Louisa-Margaretta never learned if the blush was the shame of a terrible student or the reticence of a brilliant scholar. Perhaps he would do well if he only stayed within Oxford's hallowed walls. She couldn't be bothered to find out, and his conversation was dry and exceedingly boring.

Cousin Ephraim was hardly better. Her mother had been shut up with him for an hour, begging him to allow Christmas gifts for his daughters. He seemed to feel that due to the death of his wife, nobody was to ever have a moment of fun ever again. Louisa-Margaretta could not feel sorry for him, and she did not try to remedy this fault. If he did not wish to enjoy a country Christmas, he should not have forced himself on them. She remembered asking her mother not to invite him, but apparently, Uncle Horace had begged because he had not seen Cousin Ephraim in some time. Her father had made some vague comments about how they "might do well to have a physician under their roof." But Louisa-Margaretta did not trust her cousin's expertise. Ever since his wife died, he had seen very few patients, and she imagined that his skills were not what they once were.

At first, Louisa-Margaretta had imagined that Aunt Matilda would be exactly the person their sorry little circle needed. All the men were dreary except Cousin Theo, but his complaints about the "sad, bleak country" in which he found himself were also tiring. Even Louisa-Margaretta, who had complained about Derbyshire every day since her arrival, quickly found his jokes and reminiscences trying. She asked him more than once why he had not simply stayed on the continent if England was such a sorry place in comparison, but he never really answered. At least, not seriously.

Aunt Matilda arrived the morning of December sixteenth then stayed shut in her room for what seemed like half the day. When Louisa-Margaretta tried to go after her, she found that her aunt had gone out walking. Louisa-Margaretta wished to ride, but she did not want to have to keep to her aunt's pace out of politeness. A glance out the window showed that Aunt Matilda had not gone far. She was only in the garden, speaking to Mr Bragg, her face contorted with anger. At one point, she threw off one of her gloves and stormed into the house. Louisa-Margaretta observed Mr Bragg pick up the glove, fold it, and put it in his own pocket.

Throwing down a perfectly good glove then abandoning it on the ground was hardly the mark of a lady. She knew that her aunt had not challenged the man to a duel, but she was not entirely sure what had happened.

At dinner, the conversation was not supposed to be terribly formal, as they were only a family party. But when it turned to Napoleon, the tension that had been wrapped around the group threatened to erupt.

Louisa-Margaretta, though hardly interested in the conversation, did remember some of the harsh words. But when she tried to recall all of them, that she might repeat them for the rector's daughter, Judith stopped her.

"Enough," said Judith. "We've no time for Napoleon. We both must go."

"Poppycock," said Louisa-Margaretta, glaring at her. "You were the one who claimed to need this account."

$\mathcal{H}$ 24 $\mathcal{H}$

"No," said Judith, who had been sitting exceptionally still until the sight of her bedraggled father made her spring into action. "You must get your coat. My father is returning, and he'll be very surprised indeed if he catches you here."

She could see that her father had reached the top of the hill, and she wondered if one of the troubles of Derbyshire was that it was difficult to see people approaching. It certainly made subterfuge feel completely impossible.

Her father was nearing the church with Mr Theo Ramsbury, and they were deep in conversation. There wasn't a door to the outside from the room where they were, and Judith had to lock the room first so they could leave through the sanctuary without being seen. It could have been her nerves, but it really seemed as if there were something wrong with the lock. She couldn't get the key to turn the way it usually did. In desperation, she blew on the key to make it warmer so it would turn.

"I'm not sure why you would do that," said Louisa-Margaretta, her voice chilly. "It never works."

"Something had better work," murmured Judith, pushing the key harder then with more finesse. "Merciful heavens."

Finally, she felt the lock cooperate, and she grabbed Miss Haddington by the arm. "Say you were helping me with the inventory," she said.

"Why on earth would I do that?"

"Because you need a reason to explain your presence here! Merciful heavens, no lady would want to spend five minutes in this horrid vestry. It's freezing!"

Miss Haddington, beside herself at her companion's outburst, let out a hiss of laughter just as the gentlemen entered.

"Papa," said Judith. "Mr Ramsbury."

Though she could tell Miss Haddington would have preferred to leave immediately, they could not slight the gentlemen.

"I am sorry that I was not here with you," said Judith's father, bowing his head as he looked at Miss Haddington. But his was not the deference of an inferior tugging his forelock, rather the condescension of an older and stronger being attempting to soothe a flighty female. "I understand it was a very trying morning for you. I understand why you might wish to pray, and I should have laid a fire."

"Miss Haddington was helping me with the inventory, Papa," said Judith with unaccustomed brightness in her voice, realizing as she said it that she was throwing away a very good excuse for the young lady's presence. She should have said that of course Miss Haddington was troubled, and they had prayed together, but she had been so fixated on using her little task as an excuse that she quite forgot about any useful embellishments.

"We did think to lay a fire for you," said Miss Haddington, and Judith thought that another listener might well miss the panic in her companion's voice. "You were wonderful with Mr

Bragg, truly. But Judith says you have not had tea. Should we bring some over from the rectory?"

"Surely, you should not busy yourself with such a task," said Mr Theo Ramsbury, looking animated for the first time. Though he had clearly been speaking with Judith's father intently as he came in, he had fallen silent and hardly greeted them. "Why don't you ladies keep to your work, or better still, head back to the house. Your mother was missing you, Cousin Louisa-Margaretta."

"I'm sure the servants all know I was here," she murmured. "Wilkins knew, at any rate."

"I can walk you back," said Judith. "The exercise will do me good."

When they were outside, in the open air and some distance away from the church, she looked back. "Do you think you can bear some time with your Mr Ramsbury?"

"My Cousin Theo? As enraptured as he is with the continent, he shows no sign of actually leaving our home, so I suppose I shall have to bear it."

"Yes," said Judith cautiously. "But what if you were courting?"

❧ 25 ❧

Louisa-Margaretta laughed so much that she could hardly stand. "Oh, generous Judith, don't tell me you have joined the conspiracy of ladies who all wish to find me a husband?"

Generous Judith flinched, and Louisa-Margaretta knew that she had struck her mark. Yet another person to worry about her! It was rather disappointing, really. Louisa-Margaretta had actually heard the young woman railing about women getting the vote, which was a particularly radical position in Derbyshire. She had marked little Miss Judith St Clair as someone who would be happy to see Louisa-Margaretta refuse such a mercenary arrangement. But still, she reflected, Judith was a rector's daughter. Obviously, given that she was making note of every dusty old hymnal on a morning when she could have joined a picnic or done something amusing, she was greatly devoted to the church. That was bound to influence her view of Louisa-Margaretta's decisions.

Since Judith still had not answered, Louisa-Margaretta snapped, "I am sure that if either of us needs a husband, it is you, my dear. I have the money to be a confirmed spinster, and I shall die rich. You must worry about having food on the table, or rather you should."

"Indeed, I am well aware that I may not ever leave off worrying about that. I bid you good day."

Louisa-Margaretta worried that Judith would go and tell her father of their suspicions, which would only worsen the danger. Wary of throwing her only ally into the arms of the church, even if she was an incorrigible little thing with no sense of humour, Louisa-Margaretta began to wheedle. She had never liked apologies, but the memory of shot and rocks falling on her shoulders was a fresh one.

"I'm sorry, I meant no harm. You all have every reason to wish me married, but because I do not wish it myself, it will not come off."

Judith stood still. "What, you thought I wished you to marry?"

I know you wished me to marry, thought Louisa-Margaretta. *I saw how you reacted when I declared it.*

But she did not say this aloud.

What she said instead was, "None of my conversations with my poor cousins will end in marriage, I can certainly say that much."

Judith sighed. "I do not know what will end in marriage. If you have not the inclination to marry, perhaps nothing will. But I do know that we need more insight when it comes to the gentlemen of your household. And the only way either of us will be able to speak to them with any modicum of privacy is under the guise of courtship."

Louisa-Margaretta laughed. How naive her friend was! "My dear, courtship will give us no privacy at all. Courtship means chaperones and aunts at every turn! Our movements watched! No, that is no sort of plan." She briefly remembered that she had no more aunts to watch her movement, but she brushed away the little wasp of sadness that seemed poised to sting her upon this recollection.

But Miss St Clair was stubborn. She adjusted her worn hat. It could not have ever been very fashionable, but it appeared warm. Louisa-Margaretta's own turban was lovely, but her ears were stinging in the cold winter air.

"If a lady and a gentleman walk about the grounds, particularly when they are in view of others, there is nothing very suspicious in that, is there?" Miss St Clair offered gently. "Or, perhaps, if they drink tea together with others present, or write verses. We need not be plain about our own intentions. But your cousin Mr Morgan Ramsbury will hardly speak to me, Mr Theo Ramsbury is never serious for a moment, and Mr Ephraim Ramsbury is taciturn and angry."

It was a fair summation of her three sorry cousins. To choose a husband from such a group! Impossible. Instead of three wise men, she had been presented with a mouse, a clown, and a viper.

"And what of Mr Bragg?" Louisa-Margaretta asked. "We cannot either of us court him — he's married."

"Gentlemen speak with each other," insisted Miss St Clair. "If we spend time with one of the younger ones, they will tell us about their elders. Mr Horace Ramsbury, for example."

"Uncle Horace!" she gasped. "Surely, he would never think of such a thing as murder. He is old, and he is not at all well!"

"Then he has less to lose, perhaps?"

Louisa-Margaretta shook her head. "I shall never consider him. He cannot have been the man who tried to shoot me. But if you insist, I suppose a pretence of courtship could give us some information. I have no alternative to suggest, and I do not fancy another brush with death." She kept her voice even as she said it, but for a little quaver. She noticed that Judith was watching her sharply.

"Then perhaps you would give *me* an assignment," she said quietly.

"I beg your pardon?"

"If I am to set my cap at one of your cousins, you are the best person to tell me the name of my intended target."

26

Louisa-Margaretta took to her bed when she came in and had her supper sent in on a tray. For once, she deserved an entire evening to gather her nerves. The task that Judith had set her was more abhorrent than she had first thought. Though she feared for her life, what the two of them had come up with was a profound betrayal of the only man she would ever love. And even though she was forbidden from writing to him and had no way of knowing even the tiniest thing about how he had spent the days since she left with her family, she felt as if he could see her.

"Isaac," she whispered, "I'm sorry."

The wind whistled against the panes, and even underneath the bedclothes, she shivered. She was thankful that her mother, however devoted to fresh air, prayer, brisk walks, and other pursuits, was not one of those tyrants who insisted on the whole family keeping their windows open in winter. She had always cheerfully intoned that windows one could close and open were not meant to be constantly kept in one position, and at least on that point, she and her wayward daughter could agree.

Louisa-Margaretta remembered the day that they first arrived, her father exhausted from the journey, her mother pacing the halls and seeing to the unpacking in a frenzy.

That day, she had tried to take to her bed. That seemed the only course left to her, other than perhaps not eating (which she could never manage for more than one luncheon). Mama came in and immediately made it clear that she would not be employing this little stratagem.

"Why should I not?" Louisa-Margaretta had said. "I don't care about any of the guests you've invited or about Papa or about you. You are keeping me prisoner here, and I may as well act like a prisoner. Besides, I am truly very tired, and my stomach does not feel at all well."

It was the truth, she realized. She may have generally had an iron constitution, but that afternoon, she was feeling quite off-kilter and wanted nothing more than her new bed. It was a small refuge in a house she had vowed to hate. She could not even say the name "Wycliff Castle" without dissolving in anger.

Her mother shook her head. "If you pretend to be really ill, it will only give rise to gossip. And though we will not permit you to see that young man again, how would he feel to hear that you may be dying? I am sure you would not wish to cause him distress."

In fact, Louisa-Margaretta was not sure about her wishes. In a sense, she hoped that news of her illness (though she knew that she was not ill, exactly) would reach Isaac's ears. She hoped that he would think she might be dying and that any sense of propriety that had kept him from immediately coming to the place where she lived would fall away.

But she did not wish to cause him pain, and she knew that she had when she agreed to go with her family. Of course, they had tricked her, telling her that they were going to visit her Aunt Matilda and talk the whole thing over "as a family," when they were actually journeying to Derbyshire. They knew that she would fall asleep on the carriage ride, waking only when they were so far away they could not have possibly been going to her aunt's. Regardless, she could have found a way out. They had to stop to change horses. But then, too, there had been murmurings from her mother that Aunt Matilda was far away and that only by this circuitous route could she hope for a happy conclusion.

Louisa-Margaretta did not care for her aunt, but on that journey, she had hoped her parents' desire to talk over the situation meant they had not absolutely decided against her. She would never make such a silly mistake again. It was all a great falsehood, one of too many.

And in the morning, she was to add another.

27

J udith reflected, as she shivered her way through halls that seemed far too dark, that it was a difficult thing gaining the interest of a man who did not wish to hear a thing about love or money.

She had been thinking about how to invent an ailment when she realized that she could simply use her own condition, so the next morning, she set off as early as she could for Wycliff Castle so that she might consult Mr Ephraim Ramsbury. After all, Judith was often cold and exhausted. She had little appetite. And for many months, she had been noticing that her memory had begun to fail her. In fact, she recognized something of herself when she passed Mr Horace Ramsbury the day before on her walk home. He had looked remarkably ill, and Judith had wondered whether it was just the winter cold or whether he was suffering from some other malady.

But on the walk to the castle, which felt triply long in the cold, she decided to bring her sister Miriam's ailment to the man's attention. There was something about disclosing her thoughts, her secrets, that did not appeal to Judith. She was not sure if he would want to rescue her upon hearing that she was ill or if it would be repulsive to him.

Judith was supposed to be waiting for Louisa-Margaretta in the morning room, but she quickly made her way to the little ad hoc schoolroom, where she knew she was likely to find Mr Ephraim Ramsbury. But when she consulted him about Miriam, he did not have the sort of reaction that she had feared. He was interested in the problem, not the person.

"You say that her ankle still troubles her?" he asked.

"Yes," she said. "Though the bone should have healed by now, or so we had all expected."

In the early days of their mourning, Miriam had gone out riding. Only they had never been able to afford a grand stable, so none of the St Clairs were fine riders. She ended up falling off the horse and breaking at least one bone, and there were some indications that her left leg had not healed properly.

Of course, she reflected, Miriam had not once winced in pain when she was dancing. When she had to accompany their father on calls to his parishioners, however, her ankle was always giving her the most horrid pain. So perhaps part of it was more to do with duty than with medicine.

"I danced with your sister," he said. "Dark hair, but eyes that were very blue."

"Everyone has blue eyes in my family except me," she said, with a little laugh. She wondered if that was something she should point out. She always thought that her own eyes, though they were large and even, were a rather muddy and unimpressive shade of brown. Certainly nothing like Miriam's eyes, which were clear and bright as if they were painted by a rather dramatic artist. Her father's eyes were closer to grey, pale but innocuous, whereas her mother's eyes had been just like Miriam's.

"And your mother?" he asked. "You have the same mother?"

She smiled. "Yes, all of us have the same mother and father. My parents married young, and we are a large family. Though there were two children lost between Miriam and our brothers, so we are in two little groups, as it were."

He nodded, frowned for a moment, then looked back at the fire.

"Well. I am happy to examine your sister's ankle, with her permission and your father's, and give recommendations. There are some exercises she can perform which may give her the strength to live with any weakness that remains."

She blinked. "Exercises? But surely, the bone has healed?"

He smiled, and she thought there was something sad in it. "Perhaps not completely. But strengthen the leg, and you can keep the pain down. It has worked well for many. She can learn to move in a way that does not upset her."

He leaned forwards, and she could see that he was not moved by her charms. Surely, he was going to make his excuses and leave. She searched frantically for a way to keep him there.

"Is this your speciality, then?" she said. "As a physician, I mean. Wounds such as my sister's?"

He shook his head. "We are in great need of research, of knowledge, such that I cannot afford to specialize in. And with so many wounded from these senseless wars, there are many areas with which I must become familiar."

"And you help them? The young men, I mean?"

A cloud passed over his face. "Well, as you know, my wife passed away just after we lost my adoptive mother. So I have stayed with my daughters and also tried to get both estates in order. When I have things settled, perhaps when my two are a bit older, I will return to my research. At present, I can spare no more than two days in ten."

It was an arrangement many would envy, thought Judith wryly. Her own father's work took him from home every single day without exception, and their use of the rectory meant that the patron expected him to be at their beck and call constantly. If there were a madman or a murder or a lady who wished to have him lead the company in a prayer, he was to come at once.

"It sounds like very interesting work," she said. "I hope your daughters appreciate its import."

They were interrupted by his uncle, Mr Horace Ramsbury, who came through the door and wrinkled his nose. "Good day, Miss St Clair. Ephraim, I had been hoping to speak with you."

"Thank you, Uncle. We have company." He nodded to Judith with the first real warmth she had noticed from him. "I can speak with you later if you'd like."

"I was hoping for this hour, specifically," he said. "As you may recall, we were to speak yesterday, but then the events of the afternoon made it impossible. And the day before, but —"

Judith heard Louisa-Margaretta's laugh from the corner, where the languorous music of her harp continued.

"Uncle," she said. "We are all staying in the same house, grand though it may be. I am sure you shall have another opportunity to speak with Cousin Ephraim, perhaps when my dear friend is not present."

The man turned positively red as he turned and left the room.

Mr Ephraim Ramsbury shook his head. "You need not have banished him," he said. "He wants to speak of his health, only not in front of the ladies. I have told him that there is little to be done, but perhaps he does not wish to believe me."

At this, the harp music stopped, and Louisa-Margaretta must have forgotten that she was supposed to be fading away during a tête-à-tête between her "dear friend" Judith and her cousin. She came rushing over.

"Surely, Uncle Horace isn't poorly!" she said. "You can't mean that."

"I'm sure that nobody could mistake him for a man who is well," said her cousin, meeting her eyes and giving a hint of a shrug of his shoulders. "Miss St Clair, you met our uncle quite recently. Did he seem quite well to you?"

She could feel herself turning pink at his inquiring gaze, and Judith's glare grew cold and demanding. "Well, I did not see much of him, really. Just at the ball then after the shoot, of course."

"But would you have thought he was a man who was quite well?"

"No," Judith said quietly. "No, I do not believe so."

"Well then, cousin," he said to Louisa-Margaretta. "Our uncle has lived a full life, and it was long. And he may have some time yet. But as to a cure, I cannot offer one. He does not have the sort of condition that can be cured."

Louisa-Margaretta seemed to remember that her place was supposed to be at the harp. "Well," she said, casting her gaze towards the back of the room. "Perhaps I shall return to my music."

Judith noticed for the first time that Louisa-Margaretta's eyes were rather like her own. But how different those muddy eyes looked in a fine face, and on a young woman so tall she was eye to eye with many of the men in the party. Louisa-Margaretta greatly resembled her own mother, who was a formidable figure in many ways.

The next piece on the harp was decidedly melancholy ("Lo, How a Rose E'er Blooming"), and she gave an inward sigh at her friend's sentimentality. Louisa-Margaretta Haddington was going to get lost in worry for her uncle and thoughts of life's inevitable end. She was also playing softly, with romance in her air, no doubt to ensure that the easily trapped Mr Ephraim Ramsbury would look at the enticing Judith with something more than polite interest. Louisa-Margaretta's penchant for romance was meant to keep the gentleman from being on his guard about the murder.

"It is a difficult time to contemplate leaving this life," Judith said firmly. "Indeed, there are a great deal of things unsettled in the world. It would feel strange to put one's affairs in order, or try to, with so much uncertainty."

"Your father has doubtless read to you from Revelation," said Mr Ramsbury, and Judith tried to stifle a laugh.

Revelation, though apparently beloved by Louisa-Margaretta's mother, was not one of her father's favourite books. He was wont to say, "All generations think they are living through end days, my dear" whenever she brought it up. In fact, he rarely strayed from the Old Testament. When he did, it was generally to speak of Jesus's regard for the poor, not the strangely specific details of the apocalypse.

"What puts you in mind of Revelation, Mr Ramsbury?" she asked.

"Well," he said. "The Luddites, for one."

"Yes," she said, shuddering. "Imagine spending such sums on machines, only to see them smashed. It is as if some cannot understand progress."

Judith herself often wished she could design machines. She had a mind for figures and thought that she might make a good job of it. But she found the idea of people destroying such marvels of human invention a horrifying one.

She succeeded only in hearing a bitter laugh. "Yes, I'm sure the Haddingtons and their like hate to hear anything about the Luddites."

The harp music slowed. Judith reached forwards to take her teacup and threw a glance at her friend. She hoped Louisa-Margaretta would be able to read the expression in her eyes, because she could not gesture with her hands without alerting Mr Ramsbury.

"What do you mean, sir?" she managed, silently ordering Louisa-Margaretta to stay quiet.

"Well, only that workers want to be able to eat and to live in homes that are not filthy. If there were any other protections for their livelihoods besides destroying machines and writing poems about men who probably don't exist, I'm quite sure they would reach for those. But the owners of the machines themselves do not wish to share even a tiny piece of the profits, and so the workers are under threat. Mr Haddington's business interests are not safe from the Luddites," he said. "And truly, when we think of the forces they are fighting, we should all be on our guard."

Judith considered her response. Apparently, Mr Ephraim Ramsbury would only converse on the subject of maladies physical and political, and she must try to hold his interest.

"You sound rather like a continental radical, I think," she said. She did not dare tell the man that he sounded like Napoleon, but he spoke with a fury that seemed hardly justified.

"Somehow, we have convinced ourselves that it is radical to posit that human beings deserve to live dignified lives of labour and rest," he said. "I do not find that idea particularly radical myself."

Then, getting some handle on his anger, he cleared his throat.

"What is your own opinion?"

"I suppose," she said, "I do not like the violence of it."

He nodded. "Nor do I. But as long as we ignore the concerns that are beneath, the violence will continue."

Judith shivered. She had started to feel cold again, and she took a rather unladylike gulp of tea. "Well," she said. "Perhaps

I have kept you long enough. Thank you so much for consulting with me."

"Tell your sister of my offer," he said. "Truly. I have not been able to help in this household so much as I should like, and your father has been doing the lion's share of the work. I had ideas about Mr Bragg's ailment, and I have tried the remedies available to me, but your father's mere presence has been much more helpful for that gentleman's condition."

Judith wondered whether he was sincere in his desire to help. After all, he had just been saying that the Haddingtons had better watch out for their ill-gotten gains due to some kind of Luddite incursion. Would he truly wish to assist such a family, even if they were bound by blood?

"I am sure she will be interested," she said. "But at times, she does not like to speak of the pain, so I will send word if she would like you to come for a visit."

"Very well," he said, and they both heard Agnes calling to him from down the hall. After he left, she heard him answer in the gentle tones he reserved only for his daughters.

❦ 28 ❦

Judith had time to whisper only a few words to Louisa-Margaretta as they searched the house for Mr Morgan Ramsbury. Both had decided that Mr Theo Ramsbury, since he was already inclined to talk, would not be the object of their attention. Louisa-Margaretta had confessed that she knew her cousin usually only seduced young women who could not be called gentlewomen, but she feared in his boredom, he might be less than scrupulous, particularly if either of them appeared to express a genuine regard. And this endeavour ending in an actual fit of lovemaking was something that neither of them wished to contemplate for long.

They had decided instead that Louisa-Margaretta would start paying attention to Cousin Morgan. And though the day seemed to be ending, she thought she could manage to see him before supper and to keep Judith with her.

"I should really tell Papa," Judith murmured. "I wouldn't like to keep the family waiting for me."

"What, isn't he here?" said Louisa-Margaretta, looking down the corridor where she knew her cousin's bedroom was situated. She doubted the family would be changing for dinner, not after the horrid distraction of Mr Bragg's outburst. Exasperated, she looked out the window as if she might find her cousin in the sky.

"It is a beautiful sunset," said Judith wistfully.

"Yes, another day gone and things only getting worse in this place," murmured Louisa-Margaretta. "There will be plenty of time for waxing poetic about purples and golds when we find the man we are seeking!"

They found him in the front hall, just coming in from a walk. Louisa-Margaretta pressed him to go outside again. She asked a servant for her coat before he could refuse.

"It is really rather cold," he said, hesitating. He looked over at Judith. "Miss St Clair, would you not be cold?"

"Perhaps, but I am made of heartier stuff," insisted Louisa-Margaretta, leaving Judith no chance to answer. As soon as she got into the coat that a servant promptly presented to her, she took her cousin's arm. "Out with you, Cousin Morgan! I do not wish to waste this sunset. Soon, it will be gone, and we shall be left with another interminable Derbyshire night."

As they stood on the front steps, he bit his lip. "You said you did not wish to waste it. Do you have designs on it, then? Have you brought your sketchbook?"

She smiled at this. If only she were a better artist, she could have taken his likeness! She knew that this was a very common way of expressing respectable interest in a gentleman. However, she had never bothered much with sketching, and as a result, anything she did come up with would invariably be insulting.

She was thankful, then, that she had a way with words.

"I am sketching it, in a sense," she said. "I will write verses and present them to you. I have always loved writing poetry."

He looked back at the door. "Did your friend not wish to join us?"

"Oh, she is so very prone to chills," said Louisa-Margaretta. "She is such a thin little thing. And she does not write poetry, so if she misses these colours, it will be no great loss."

"That seems rather unfeeling," he said.

"On the contrary!" Louisa-Margaretta cried. "I am trying to tell you that I feel all the colours very deeply. The gold of sunsets covers up the pink / That melts the hills to darkness, even now. / I tell my poor heart ne'er again to think / Of you, beloved, but I know not how."

They were not her most elegant lines, but her heart did ache when she said them. She had developed an inability to write about anything but Isaac. Every song she played on the harp, she dedicated to him in her mind, and she tended to choose only melancholy ones. Every poem was about him, for him, written as if he were standing near her. Every picturesque scene was meant to be shared with him, and she felt a rush of temper that it was her intensely ordinary cousin who stood beside her in his stead.

"Do let us go in," she said, rather shortly. He seemed little affected by her verses. In fact, he had been eyeing the door, and she was exasperated that he could not tolerate the cold. Surely, his clothing was more practical than hers, and yet she could have stayed on the steps for another half hour if she had got anything useful from him. She had hoped at least to ask what he knew of Aunt Matilda's past and what his own aims were at Oxford.

The family appeared to be gathering just inside the doors. She wondered if her brief interlude with her cousin had caused any alarm. If her parents had known about the attempt on her life, they would likely be trying to keep her between the two of them at all times, or possibly locked away in a different county. As it was, her father seemed preoccupied but not scared, exactly.

"The two of you having a nice time together, what?" he said. "I am very glad, my dear. Very glad."

And after a hearty pressure on Louisa-Margaretta's shoulder, he was off again. She looked about, but as Cousin Morgan had already disappeared, she wondered who her father had meant when he said "you two." He had looked genuinely pleased.

Uncle Horace reappeared, rushing over to his nephew. "Ephraim! I have been waiting all day to speak with you. Come, my boy."

It was an odd choice of words. Ephraim could hardly have looked less like a boy. His hair was turning grey, his face thin and strained. He nodded to his uncle, but at that moment, they heard footsteps on the drive.

The footsteps of more than one person. As the footsteps drew closer, they heard singing. It was women singing, only women, and their voices might have been beautiful had Louisa-Margaretta not been horrified to see her efforts interrupted. Judith, wringing her hands, also looked put out.

Mr Horace Ramsbury looked even more upset. His face was pink again. "Oh, Hell and the Devil," he said. "Let the women see them, Ephraim, and come speak with me. There are too many widows in this county for all of them to come here."

It was a boorish remark, and even Louisa-Margaretta looked alarmed. "Uncle Horace," she managed.

Ephraim's face looked even more strained. "Yes, they have lost the ones they married," he said. "But you would claim that these ladies are not deserving of notice or, heaven forbid, of pity."

His uncle was nearly panicked. "Dash it all, I did not

mean — surely, you know that, for you — please come and sit with me, Ephraim."

Louisa-Margaretta thought she had seen the cold face Mr Ephraim Ramsbury put on when he was not impressed with his company. As it turned out, she had not.

The chill in his face as he turned away from his uncle was quite different. Though when the doors were opened, he managed warmth, even a smile, for the widows who came through them.

It was St Thomas Day. They had all forgotten.

The cook, it appeared, had not. There was plenty of cooked wheat at hand, and Mrs Haddington was quite excited to have both her daughter and "dear Miss St Clair" assist her in sharing it with the mumpers. She also insisted on giving out apples. Though she disliked wassail, apples might be presents not only for revellers but for children. One need not assume that they would be used for strong drink.

Louisa-Margaretta was tapping her foot before the gathering was half over. She achieved some degree of privacy with Cousin Morgan, who had probably returned so as not to seem rude, as the attention of the room was turned away from them.

"I suppose we must consider the widows," she said. "But I do wish they would not sing half so many songs."

She had hoped to make her taciturn cousin laugh, but he only shook his head.

"Poor things," he said. "We really ought to do more for women. Then we would worry less for the widows."

Louisa-Margaretta peered at him, feeling that he might have made some sort of obscure accusation. She wondered whether he shared Judith's passion for giving women the vote. She herself thought it all sounded very dull. "Most women do not have independent means," she said. "If I do not end a widow but only an unmarried woman, I shall have very little of my own."

She wondered for a moment whether she ought to have raised that possibility. After all, she was supposed to be spinning tales of how she might marry her cousin, not how she was going to end her days unmarried. In spite of her devotion to her vow of spinsterhood, she knew she could not keep sharing it with members of her family without becoming an object of ridicule. But if she and Isaac did not marry, she would never marry. She was quite sure of that.

"You have had the benefit of an excellent education, cousin," he said, still not looking at her. She wondered which mumper it was who caught his eye then felt ashamed. Though some of the widows being served wheat were beautiful, none of them had independent means if they had walked all the way to the house to sing for such a measly portion of food. And it was not even good food — Louisa-Margaretta had always detested wheat, making the lumpy spoonfuls that her mother and Judith were doling out seem all the sorrier. Perhaps she should convince her parents to give out joints of meat next St Thomas Day if she was still living with them.

She started. She would not be living with them, surely! She meant to leave Wycliff Castle as soon as she found the murderer. She could not allow herself to consider the horrid place her home, or she risked losing her determination to go after Isaac as soon as she could reasonably escape.

"Now you sound like Cousin Ephraim," she said, trying to sound lighthearted. "He thinks everything is a matter of education, especially where his daughters are concerned."

"Well," said her cousin, turning towards her, "he is not entirely wrong there. As I said, when women are not paid fair wages, education may provide some little guard against poverty."

"Marriage is a better guard," said Louisa-Margaretta,

wondering how much easier her life would be if she had been allowed to marry where she loved. She might be married already and safe instead of trying to goad her cousin into revelations. "Education did not teach me a thing I could use for money-making, except that I now read and write well enough to be a governess, or a companion."

"You may wish to consider the other gifts education has given you," he said. "Your verses, for example. You would not be able to write those without having studied Shakespeare."

His gaze had wandered again, but she stared at him until he felt the weight of her eyes and turned towards her. "How on earth could I make money off verses?" she asked.

"You could sell them," he said simply. "People buy books of poetry daily. Why not one of yours?"

"Why would they buy a book of poetry that a woman has written? Even novels by women are outsold by those written by men."

He nodded. "I don't suppose you write novels, then?"

"Absolutely not. Mama would kill me if I attempted it. Besides, I have no patience for such a dull task."

"Not your father? He would not mind?"

"I believe Papa would think me rather enterprising."

He laughed for the first time. Some of the mumpers were still singing, but it looked as if they were going to leave soon. Louisa-Margaretta was now eyeing the wheat with longing. This display had delayed their meal, and she would have accepted anything that might quiet her hunger.

"You don't happen to like writing music, do you? Because you could set your verses to a tune, then sell that. People are always looking for a new song to sing at the pianoforte at this time of year."

She sniffed. "Well, there is very little of that in this house. And I can't come up with tunes at all. Everything I play on the harp I have learned specially."

He nodded. "It was only a thought. I am sure you will come up with your own ideas. I did not mean to press you."

She shook her head. "It does not matter. I am angry that I do not have my own fortune, but I am hardly in the same position as our Mr Bragg. Do you think he will leave his room to hear any of the music? The mumpers will be going."

Her cousin shook his head. "I hope he has managed to get some rest. I believe he has hardly slept since our aunt's passing."

Louisa-Margaretta sighed. "I cannot understand that. Is there any sense in staying up all night? It will do nothing for her spirit. It is like beating one's breast ceremonially or some other heathen ritual."

"It cannot be helped," said her cousin gently. "In times of grief, it is not unheard of. Sleep does not come. When my mother died, I did not sleep for the first night and knew little rest for months after."

Louisa-Margaretta had the grace to lower her eyes, though she still thought Mr Bragg an unconscionably rude guest. "Did others in your family sleep, though?"

He shook his head. "You will already know that my brother attempted to form an engagement around that time."

Louisa-Margaretta, who had not known, said nothing.

"Our father was against it, absolutely," he said. "And Theo was sixteen, far too young for such a thing. But he really would have gone through with it had not Papa insisted on paying off the young girl's family. They sent her away, and the engagement ended. Then he grieved, for Mama and for her, I think."

Louisa-Margaretta's heart was pounding. She looked carefully at her cousin. An old family with a reputation to uphold, an engagement broken when the young lady's family accepted a generous sum in exchange for a removal. She had never suspected her own parents of such conduct. Surely, they had taken her to Wycliff Castle of their own volition, without the interference of any mercenary motive. They had money of their own, a great deal of it! But was it as much as Isaac's family? There were rumours about the Luddites, and it was just possible that her father's business interests — but no. Her parents could not possibly have accepted money to — but if they felt that they needed it, that it would be to her benefit?

She nodded. "Well. That must have been terrible. I'm very sorry, but would you mind if I changed for dinner? I am already starving and should hate to have anyone wait for me."

Before she could leave, Judith joined her and Cousin Morgan. Louisa-Margaretta longed to hear her friend's thoughts on what she had just learned, but Judith had come only to say that the mumpers were going by the rectory, and she was going to follow them.

"Tomorrow," she whispered after she had leaned in so close to Louisa-Margaretta that nobody could hear them. "I'll be able to tell you all that I've learned. But this evening, there is no time!"

Both of them straightened up, and Louisa-Margaretta hoped that they simply seemed to be silly young ladies making a large show of an embrace as they said what was to be a very short-lived farewell. Some of her mother's friends were that way. It was as if they could not survive without Mama's company from one teatime to the next.

Judith, on the other hand, did not seem devastated to be leaving. She looked so bright as she said it that Louisa-Margaretta almost remarked that she seemed to have forgotten the purpose of their meeting. But then she realized her cousin Morgan was still standing beside her. He offered Judith his arm.

"I can go with your group as far as the rectory," he said. "It has got very dark."

Judith looked at her feet but took his arm, leaving Louisa-Margaretta even more annoyed. Her cousin could not possibly know that they were facing actual danger. Instead, he was taking every opportunity of boasting about his gallant nature when really, he would probably run back from cold when he had not gone half a mile.

29

In the morning, Louisa-Margaretta decided that she would sleep and send her breakfast away. She had no wish to meet her friend early. But instead of sleeping, she sat at her dressing table, thinking about writing verses but putting nothing down on paper. Nothing pretty would come to her. She thought only of murder.

She went to the window. It was clear that Judith's original suspicion had been correct in a general sense, but that did not bring her closer to knowing which man under her roof was a murderer.

Mr Bragg was still in hiding, having taken his supper the night before on a tray, but Louisa-Margaretta noticed that he had gone out walking again as soon as it was light. His walk, instead of containing the mad fury that had gone before, was slow. It was almost as if he were crippled. She wondered why her parents kept him about. His behaviour only annoyed her more as Christmas approached, but she was worried that she might provoke him into more violence. For with each day, she wondered whether he had been behind the attack on her. He must have shot at her head just before he staged his collapse.

The trouble was, she could not be sure quite how much of it was staged. Perhaps his latest murder attempt was the desperate act that sent him into madness. She knew that some people ended their days in little madhouses in the country, never recovering their wits. Perhaps that would be Mr Bragg's fate.

Her mother had not threatened her with that, she remembered, but the spectre of the madhouse hung over their conversations. When her parents spoke of her duty to rise each morning and entertain their guests, what she heard was how much of a burden she could be to her mama and papa. Even if they had not said it outright, they could send her to Bethlem for any reason, and she would not be able to escape. She might well perish there, her feet rotting from the cold, with no friends and nobody who would hear or understand her reasons for going so decidedly against her family's wishes.

Cousin Morgan's suggestion had been entertaining if impractical. Louisa-Margaretta had no idea how she would go about finding someone to sell her compositions to, if indeed she was able to set her verses to music. She had always been able to write her own songs, but only with a tune that was presented to her. She could not think of them on her own. The lyrics were much easier, just an extension of her poetry.

Uncle Horace had a friend who was a great frequenter of Hatchards, a London bookseller, and he was sure to know something about the process. Resolving that she would ask Uncle Horace about it, she dressed herself without ringing for help and went down to breakfast. She was dressing herself more often, or only having a maid help her for a few minutes. She did not need help with every gown, and she liked to come and go as she pleased.

Her uncle, however, waved her away when she tried to speak with him.

"No time for a chat this morning," he said gruffly. "Got to talk to my son."

"Cousin Morgan?"

"No, not him. Though I ought to speak with him as well."

He did not look particularly cheered by the prospect.

"Well, I don't know where Cousin Theo is at the moment," she said, serving herself cold eggs with false cheer. "Perhaps I could be a stand-in for him, in terms of company."

He gave her a shrewd look. "Not unless you're going to marry him. And that is not something I would advise."

She flushed, nearly dropping the slice of honey cake that she had been about to add to her plate. It was unlike her uncle to be cruel, though he was often direct. If her own uncle did not think she was suitable for marriage, what would the world at large think? Even if she wished to remain unmarried while Isaac was forbidden to her, she still had her pride. She would like to preserve her reputation as an accomplished and respectable woman.

He misinterpreted her pink cheeks. "Fallen in love with him, have you? Well, you can't marry. I wouldn't give my blessing, not that it matters this time, the parties being of age. Tried it once, and it was a mistake, perhaps. But it would have been a mistake either way! The lad was only just sixteen, and he had lost his mother."

She started. The whole scandal of Theo's first engagement, broken up by the families of the young people, had been hidden from her for nearly two decades, and in this brief little visit, she had already heard the story twice.

"I am not in love with him," she said stoutly. And that much was true. Though if she was perfectly honest, she could admit that she had enjoyed her cousin's company at times. His life was one of adventure and art. It seemed about as far removed from an isolated Derbyshire castle as it was possible for an English man of means. Or some means, rather. Mr

Horace Ramsbury had always kept a close eye on the purse. His sons were given an allowance that should allow them many amusements, but it always seemed that Cousin Theo must have been spending money from another source as well.

"Well, well," Uncle Horace said. "You're young, got many years ahead of you."

If another person had said it, it would have been a joke, but Uncle Horace appeared perfectly serious.

And with that, he left the room.

Louisa-Margaretta hardly touched her breakfast. She had thought Mr Bragg mad, but seeing her Uncle Horace was worse. A man who had always been gentle in his manners and respectful in his tone was now bitter and rude. Surely his illness alone could not account for it. She knew that Cousin Ephraim, as a physician, did not give him much time, but he had not said anything about madness.

Slowly, she began to recall the evening of the ball. When Aunt Matilda had been addressing the assembled company, Louisa-Margaretta had once looked over at her Uncle Horace and noticed that his face was red, his fists clenched. At the time, she thought it was simply because Aunt Matilda was drunk, which was not particularly forgivable in a lady. She expected that Uncle Horace was angry simply because such behaviour reflected poorly on the family. But now, she began to wonder whether there might have been something else behind his rage and whether he had acted on it by going after Aunt Matilda and ending her life.

Shaking her head, she pushed her plate away. She needed to get word to her friend. But looking outside, she saw that the wind and cold threatened. The ground remained bare, but she still felt the possibility of snow keenly.

It would be wise to take a horse.

❦ 30 ❦

When Judith saw Louisa-Margaretta riding up to the rectory, looking as if she were in a royal procession, she wondered what had got into her friend.

It was not a long walk, and even a carriage would have been less strange. But Louisa-Margaretta appeared in a hurry. It was not a decent hour for a social call, but she must have had some excuse prepared for any family member who questioned her early excursion.

Before Judith could ask, Aunt Leah had come to greet Louisa-Margaretta. She was up early with the boys, as she often was of late. Judith, who had felt the duty of rising early with her brothers ever since their mother's death, had slept more after meeting the Haddingtons. Balls, mumpers, suppers that went well into the night. The wealthy family seemed to make a virtue of staying up and could sleep when they liked, and to Judith's shame, she had found herself still abed many mornings as the rest of the household stirred around her. Sloth was a fault she would certainly need to work hard in order to remedy. It did not suit her.

This morning, however, she had not slept well and had made her way downstairs quite early, hoping that playing Bach on the pianoforte would be soothing. Miriam was still asleep, but she slept soundly and would not complain until she was awake anyway. She turned up her nose at Judith's music, finding it cold and technical, always begging for a cheerful jig or a romantic adagio.

And so Judith found herself sitting in the parlour with Aunt Leah and a rather prim Louisa-Margaretta, making polite conversation about the preparations for Christmas Day and the performances of the mumpers the previous evening.

"I was hoping," said Louisa-Margaretta, "that is, I should be quite honoured if you would join us for tea this evening, Miss St Clair."

Aunt Leah betrayed more surprise than was entirely polite. "Are you quite sure? We would not wish to intrude upon your family."

"It is not an intrusion, truly, because your company is welcome. I must admit, we have none of us been feeling particularly festive."

"And you think the company of your rector, his unmarried sister, and his two irreverent daughters will cheer you? We are poor substitutes for your London friends, I am sure."

"Not at all," said Louisa-Margaretta simply. "Friends are friends."

It was a truly excellent statement, as Aunt Leah was not able to easily make any response. She only managed, "One of us will have to stay home with the boys, of course."

"Could not a servant stay with them?" said Louisa-Margaretta. "After all, Wycliff Castle is only a stone's throw from the rectory. One or all of you could easily return if you were needed."

Aunt Leah shifted. "I would not say it is a stone's throw away. Though I am not in the habit of throwing stones."

Judith frowned. She had never associated rudeness with her aunt and was sure that Aunt Leah might force the hostess to rescind the invitation. Surely, Aunt Leah would not want to threaten the very living that was responsible for the fire crackling before them? It was a fire to which they were all drawn in spite of the dictates of politeness, their chairs inching ever closer like particularly sly little barn cats inching towards a delicious mouse.

"As I mentioned, the company of friends would be greatly cheering," said Louisa-Margaretta firmly, and Judith noted with some satisfaction that Aunt Leah had underestimated the power of a young woman who was very much used to getting her way. "Perhaps one of you might stay here, but I hope very much that the other three shall honour us with their company. My mother and I shall expect you at seven."

Aunt Leah, however, was also holding firm.

"Oh, your dear mother," she managed. "I am very sure I would not wish to give offense, but neither would I wish to burden her during this time. It is all very trying, to be sure."

"Our yoke is easy, our burden is light," quoted Louisa-Margaretta. "Miss St Clair, would it be a great deal of trouble if you were to show me out? I wanted to show off the bay. I think she would be a good mount for you."

When they were outside, examining the horse, Louisa-Margaretta took Judith's arm. "You'll be dragging your aunt here over every objection," she said. "See to it that she comes, and your father, too."

"Why?" said Judith. "I would like everyone in my family to be safe. I'll have to make an excuse for Miriam to stay home with the boys, and really, I would prefer that Papa not join us."

"He must," snapped Louisa-Margaretta. "Mr Bragg is worse, and nobody can speak with him except your papa.

Besides, the visit will be a distraction. You and I need to speak to Uncle Horace. He has been . . . well, worrying me."

Judith saw Aunt Leah looking out the window. Her polite smile had been replaced by a rather cross expression. Judith lowered her voice.

"You told me there was nothing wrong with your uncle," she said. "You promised! Said it would be completely out of character for him to be violent, and besides, he couldn't have had any expectation that he might benefit from your aunt's death."

"His words are violent," said Louisa-Margaretta firmly. "And they never were before, so something has certainly come over him. I hate to think of him doing it. I want it to be Mr Bragg, but I can no longer assure you of his innocence. You and I must speak to him and find out where he was when the shots were fired at me. If he did it, he must have killed my aunt as well."

Judith put her hand on the horse's flank, and the animal sidestepped her. She took a sharp step back.

"Easy, dear," said Louisa-Margaretta. "Judith, is there a mounting block nearby?"

Judith's look was blank, and Louisa-Margaretta mounted the horse easily when she remembered that the other young lady was not in the habit of riding. Louisa-Margaretta soon got the bay under control, though the horse danced a bit at first.

"I do not think that horse would suit me at all," said Judith. "Whatever possessed you of that idea?"

"I wished that you would come out and see me off, dear friend," said Louisa-Margaretta, not lowering her voice at all and with a pointed smile towards the window where Aunt Leah still stood, her eyes flashing. "My mother and I are very much looking forward to this evening."

And she was off, riding away from Judith's new home back towards her own.

Judith's stomach clenched with worry. She must find a way to be absolutely certain that both her aunt and her father joined her in the evening. As little as she liked the plan, she could not go on wondering.

It was time to draw out the murderer.

Judith could not help feeling a familiar sensation of awe as she, her father, and her aunt approached Wycliff Castle. Aunt Leah, after her brother persuaded her to attend the tea, had not once criticized the family. But as they slowly approached the grand home, she could not help saying to Judith, "Really too large a house for one family, is it not? Even a wealthy family with any number of cousins visiting for Christmas."

The house loomed large in the moonlight. It seemed beautiful and calm, almost as if its character had not been at all affected by the horrible events within its rooms.

Judith sighed. "Well, we can be thankful that it is not our home, then."

"Yes. Instead, you can wake everyone in the rectory with your early-morning Bach."

"I did not wake anyone. Only Miriam was still sleeping, and my playing does not disturb her."

"Being left out of the invitation disturbed her quite a bit. What did you say your Miss Haddington's reason was?"

"Well," she said. "She did not wish Miriam away, truly, but

she recalled the necessity of leaving someone behind to watch the boys, and of course, Papa is the only one who seems able to help with one of their guests. Our hostess felt that it might be distressing for Miriam to witness this person's, er, condition."

This was a lie. Miriam had been included in the invitation. It was Judith who, wishing to keep her sister out of danger, had said to Miriam that she could not go.

"Mr Bragg, you mean. The one who went mad while he was shooting."

Judith stared at Aunt Leah, wondering why her papa did not raise any objection, until she saw that he had been left behind. He was examining a bush by the roadside. Judith put a hand on her aunt's arm to slow her.

"How did you know that he went mad when he was shooting?" she asked, hoping that her aunt's answer would help shed light on some hitherto unknown source of information. Perhaps Mr Bragg had gone into the village, or perhaps madness ran in his family and this was common knowledge. If so, it could easily be the reason he had turned to murder.

Aunt Leah was shaking her head. "My dear niece, do you see so few similarities between this village and the one in which you spent most of your life? Everyone knows what happened on the shoot. It is the first topic of conversation around every hearth in the village and has eclipsed even poor Miss Ross's death as a first-rate curiosity."

With that, Judith felt a flush of pity as they approached the grand house. In spite of its many rooms, tasteful furnishings, and exquisite grounds, its inhabitants appeared to have less privacy than anyone around them. Miriam had breathed that in such a home, it would be possible to live "like a queen," but Judith had considered the darker side of the expression. A queen would know that her life was not private, that many of her dearest wishes were controlled entirely by others, and that even her life could never be completely safe.

Yes, perhaps one could compare the Haddingtons to royalty.

Her papa caught up as they approached the house, and she took his arm. "You will be careful, Papa, with Mr Bragg? See that there is a servant with you."

"Be easy, my dear," he said. "There is no cause for worry. I know he does not seem to be the easiest of men, but he suffers, as we did. I have nothing to fear."

Judith did not agree. One did not go about shooting at young ladies simply because one was "suffering" at the time. But she did not have time to dwell on her thoughts, as they were approaching the doors, and she knew that they would soon have to contend with Mrs Haddington's inimitable enthusiasm.

32

To her surprise, they were not to drink tea with only Mrs Haddington and Miss Haddington. The whole family had turned out for the little affair. Everyone, that is, except for Mr Bragg. Then Judith remembered that Mr Bragg was not part of the family. In fact, Louisa-Margaretta had never been able to explain why exactly he was spending Christmas at Wycliff Castle.

Judith had just turned to her father, ready to ask if he would go and see the invalid, when Mrs Haddington pressed herself upon them.

"Dear Miss St Clair," she said to Judith. "I remembered you this morning in my prayers! And how is your dear sister, and both of your brothers? You are so fortunate to live with such spirited siblings. I was the youngest of ten myself, and it was always quite lively at Christmastime, I can promise you!"

Judith felt a little more sympathy on learning that Mrs Haddington had nine older siblings. Like Louisa-Margaretta, she was the youngest and therefore had enjoyed the benefit of many playmates without ever having to show consideration for a child younger than herself. Perhaps it explained why Mrs

Haddington fully expected everyone to listen to her at every moment and why she could not stand to be silent or even reserved.

"Dear Cousin Ephraim," she said. "Pray escort our Miss St Clair to the music room. I shall be along in a bit to serve the tea, only I want to show her papa where our dear Mr Bragg has been."

After a very warm greeting for Aunt Leah, Mrs Haddington bustled off without a hint of shame. Perhaps she correctly surmised that Mr Bragg's condition was so generally known that the gossip would follow whether she alluded to it or not.

Mr Ephraim Ramsbury offered his arm, though without offering any kind words. Nevertheless, Judith blushed as she realized the plan she and Louisa-Margaretta had concocted might be starting to take effect. If Mrs Haddington believed Mr Ephraim Ramsbury was partial to Judith, she would be thinking of ways to throw them together while obeying the dictates of respectability.

"I am sure you know the way to the music room by now," he said. "The house may be large, but its arrangements are simple given its size."

"Yes," said Judith. "But I am sure we may speak as we are walking. How do your daughters fare?"

He gave a bark of a laugh. "They are missing all the things they loved about Christmas in the city. I believe they were promised ponies and snow, and as it happens, there are no ponies here, only rather wild horses. And I have not seen a single snowflake fall our whole time here."

"Well, I am sure they shall endeavour to make the best of things," Judith said, trying to keep up with him as he stalked down the hall. Indeed, she was not so much gaining support from his arm as being pulled at a run down an unfamiliar hallway, ahead of the rest of the party. "They are dear girls, after all."

He gave a little nod. "Yes. I cannot think why I brought them here."

Judith slowed her own pace, fairly dragging him to a stop. "You must pardon me," she said. "But that is abominably rude to your hostess. She has been nothing but kind, and it is hardly her fault that your Aunt Matilda passed away during your visit. I'm sure her death is more than an inconvenience."

He pulled his arm away, unsettled. "My daughters lost their mother a year ago," he said. "And I lost my wife. Is not that reason enough to wish them far from death?"

"I lost my own mother," she said. "And if I am to be perfectly honest, there are things that I prefer to a late-evening cup of tea taken in the house of gentlemen who show very little consideration for me or for my family. But I am accepting it, because I believe the Haddington family worthy of consideration. And I hope my mother would be ashamed if her death made me permanently forget my manners."

With that, she walked ahead and entered the music room alone, the first person to reach the destination of the little party. Taking one of the seats closest to the fire, she stared into the flames, hoping very much that she would find a way to make the evening pass quickly.

Mr Ephraim Ramsbury did not immediately appear, but Louisa-Margaretta soon followed with Mr Morgan Ramsbury. As they entered the room, he stole a glance at Judith, and their voices fell.

She peered at the pair of them, wondering what it was that they did not wish her to hear. Louisa-Margaretta, she noticed, had taken her cousin's arm. And unlike Judith, she had apparently not thrown herself away from the gentleman escorting her in a fit of pique.

"Dear Miss St Clair," she called. "Come and hear what plans we have been making for Christmas."

Judith gave a tight smile. She could not have given a reason, but she wished to avoid both Louisa-Margaretta and her cousin. "It is warm by the fire," she answered. "Perhaps we might persuade you to play something on the harp? It is the music room, after all."

Louisa-Margaretta rolled her eyes. "Yes, of course," she replied, and Mr Morgan Ramsbury looked a bit lost. "Come, Cousin Morgan," she said. "You are the only person in this family who doesn't get completely lost when turning pages."

He followed her like a lost lamb, looking about the room the whole time. Judith wondered why he was allowing himself to be ordered about.

Still, she stayed by the fire, uneasy. She was supposed to be speaking with Mr Horace Ramsbury. As an outsider, she might reasonably be supposed a better judge of his condition. Perhaps he was both ill and mad and had decided that it was his role as supreme judge to rid the family of people he did not like. Or perhaps he was simply ill and meant nobody any harm.

Aunt Leah came at last, taking a seat next to Judith. "Where has everyone gone?" she said, a bit cross. "We are the guests. Perhaps we are never to have tea."

"Mr Ephraim Ramsbury was out in the hallway," said Judith, knowing that she could not tell her aunt she had driven him away. Aunt Leah might grumble about the Haddingtons all she liked, but she would never be so openly rude to one of their hosts in their own house, particularly a gentleman. It was rather ironic that in scolding a man for his rudeness to Mrs Haddington, Judith had ruined the kind woman's little gathering.

"And the others? I was under the impression it was a rather large party."

"Well, nobody seems certain about Mr Horace Ramsbury. Papa and Mrs Haddington went off to find Mr Bragg, but I am not sure whether they succeeded."

Judith looked over at the fine china, wistful. Without their hostess, it seemed as if neither aim of the gathering was to succeed. She would not enjoy tea or company, and she would not gather any information on the killer.

She only hoped that her father, unbeknownst even to himself, was having greater success.

At least, she reflected, she could enjoy the fire. Though she had already warmed considerably after their walk, the fire was an even greater comfort. She wondered if it would be decent to stand near the fire but knew that she was not supposed to reveal her discomfort to her hostess. Still, as she rubbed her hands together through her gloves, she felt that the fireplace was a better feature than any of the expensive instruments. "Miss St Clair," she heard from the other side of the room. "Do come over and tell me what the markings mean! I am hopeless with Italian."

She tried to suppress a sigh as she got to her feet. She was to leave the fire, then, and tell Louisa-Margaretta that "forte" meant "loud" or some such thing.

Her task was little better. "Allegro ma non troppo," said her friend, her whole face scrunched up. "What, isn't that some sort of allegro, then? Just play it quickly."

"No," said Judith and Mr Morgan Ramsbury at the exact same time. They looked at each other then away.

Louisa-Margaretta sat straighter. "Well then, give me an explanation. We may as well embrace all of the instruments in this room, as there's no telling when Mama will think to come in and pour the tea."

"Do you play?" asked Mr Morgan Ramsbury.

There was a pause before Judith realized that the question was addressed to her. Of course it was a question for her!

Louisa-Margaretta had already been playing. Mr Morgan Ramsbury must think her rather slow. She must hope that he could not guess any more of her thoughts.

"Yes," said Judith quietly. "Since I was very young."

"Will you accompany me? Oh, do go on," said Louisa-Margaretta, which annoyed Judith. She did not consider herself an accompanist.

"My dears," said Mrs Haddington, sweeping into the room. "Thank you ever so much for waiting. As you know, a visit from our dear rector is ever so comforting for dear Mr Bragg."

Briefly, Judith thought that Mrs Haddington must never have met anyone who wasn't "dear" to her.

"I will pour the tea shortly," she said. "But first, I wanted us all to partake in one of our dearest Christmas traditions. It's much better than these silly games, Hide the Slipper, that sort of thing."

Louisa-Margaretta had briefly sat straighter on her stool, and Judith wondered if she was wishing for a childish Christmas game. It might have been a great deal more fun than trying to entertain guests and track down a killer.

"Only, we need to have everyone here," Mrs Haddington said. "Come, Louisa-Margaretta, darling, you remember this one. We all must stand in a circle. I've asked the rector to bring Mr Bragg to join us, but I'm not sure whether he shall manage it. The rest of us must all be present."

She said it so firmly that Judith wondered why all of the other members of the household did not appear on the spot. Mrs Haddington nodded, surveying the room.

"Louisa-Margaretta, go and find your father. And dear Ephraim, you have come! You should do the same — find your father, will you? And Morgan, you can come with me by the fireside and give our guests a proper welcome."

She sat down next to Aunt Leah as though nothing could

have pleased her more. "Miss St Clair, do you mean to stay long in Derbyshire?"

Nobody in the room bothered to correct her, though Judith did see Mr Morgan Ramsbury look askance for a brief moment, perhaps pondering whether he had been the one who was supposed to look for his father. After all, Mr Ephraim Ramsbury's adopted father was no longer living. But since he seemed quite eager to leave, he was the one to go out of the room, and soon, the party was down to three ladies and a gentleman.

Her child and nephews thus dispatched, Mrs Haddington settled in for a conversation, sitting rather too close and pressing Judith's arm in what some might have called an affectionate manner. Mrs Haddington had an unsettling habit of looking as if she knew very well what the hidden message was in every sentence. It could make even the lightest conversation feel frightening.

"I hope to see my nieces and nephews settled," said Aunt Leah, and Mrs Haddington nodded emphatically.

"Yes, my dear. Yes, of course."

It was as if by "settled," Aunt Leah had said "married off to rich men." It was a fiction that she wished to see her nephews settled, they were so young that it would be many years before they needed to think a great deal about their adult lives. Miriam and Judith, on the other hand, could marry. But that was not likely, not in present company. Their isolated little hamlet of Derbyshire did not offer many eligible gentlemen. Most of the people in their circle were quite poor, and Mrs Haddington's relations were all far too rich, even the ones who were considered to be poor by their own circle. Mr Morgan Ramsbury might be a second son, and Mr Ephraim Ramsbury may not have inherited as much from his adopted father as Mr Theo Ramsbury would someday inherit, but they were all in possession of storied family history and of wealth that seemed far out of Miriam and Judith's reach. They were not nearly as rich as the Haddingtons, to be sure, but neither were they in the precarious sphere that the St Clairs continued to inhabit. Miriam might do well, thought Judith, but it was wise for her father to keep her isolated in the countryside until she was a bit older. To Judith, the risk of Miriam losing her head in the city was far higher than that of her losing her bloom as she waited to return to a more lively area. In the city, with more balls and parties, Miriam might easily think of little else.

She had little time to worry about her sister, though, because Mr Theo Ramsbury had burst through the door, holding strange objects in his hands.

"Good evening, ladies," he said. "Well met, Miss St Clair and Miss St Clair! It is excellent that you have come."

Mrs Haddington frowned. "Dearest Theo," she said, "come join us by the fire. When the whole family is gathered, we are going to make a circle for a carol and some prayers."

"More like an hour of prayers, Auntie," he said. "It is nearly Christmas, and I have everything we need for snapdragon! We have a great deal of brandy and can play as many rounds as you like."

Aunt Leah smiled, barely surpassing a smirk, and Mr Morgan Ramsbury walked over to his brother.

"Dear Theo," he said. "Is it not a bit late for such games? Our aunt had her own plans for tonight's entertainment."

"The lateness of the hour is entirely the point, brother," he said. "When our cousins arrive, we shall snuff out half the candles, and the darkness will allow the flames of the brandy to glow. And then, it will be ever so hard to find the raisins!"

"Young people do like their amusements," said Aunt Leah.

"Come, Miss St Clair," said Mr Theo Ramsbury, taking Judith's hand and dragging her over to the table where he had set down a bowl of raisins. He took a great swig of the brandy before he poured it over them.

"Miss St Clair, would you not play for us?" said Mr Morgan Ramsbury. "Indeed, I know we have been importuning you, but I truly wish —"

"Surely, Miss St Clair would not prefer the pianoforte to a good game of snapdragon!" shouted Mr Theo Ramsbury, and Judith wondered if he had sampled the brandy before he came into the room.

"You may not be sure of my preferences, Mr Ramsbury, as you have not taken the trouble of asking me," she said archly. "But since it has been the general request of the party, I will play."

Abandoning the gentleman with the bowl of brandy, she sat down at the pianoforte, and though she would have found great comfort in Bach, she knew she must play the festive tunes of the season. She chose Handel, therefore, since in that way, she could play something that would cheer the company while still being allowed to choose music that was dignified rather than wild.

Mr Theo Ramsbury had already begun snuffing candles out. "I suppose I may end up with badly burned hands if I must get all the raisins on my own," he said. "But such is my fate."

Mrs Haddington was now out of her seat. "Theo, dearest," she said. "We really should wait until everyone has had tea. I will pour it now, but if the water has gone cold, you will need to ask for more."

"Some invitation this was, with no tea at all! It is just as well that I brought the brandy. I'm just trying to entertain your guests for you, Aunt. You should be thanking me."

At this, she sighed. "My dear, my dear. Perhaps you could go and find —"

He used a candle to light the brandy, and Judith gazed at it for a moment. In spite of Mr Ramsbury's mad assurances, she had to find herself agreeing with his promise. The flaming brandy was, indeed, rather beautiful.

But even the man who had set the fire had no time to grab for a single raisin. At that moment, Mr Ephraim Ramsbury walked through the door. "You must come quickly," he said.

His words were vague, but the sight of him quieted the company. Mrs Haddington went to him right away, and even Mr Theo Ramsbury stepped away from the flaming bowl of brandy and raisins.

"Why?" asked Judith, beset by a sense of foreboding. Her hands had frozen on the keys of the pianoforte, where she had stopped mid-bar.

"My uncle is dead."

꙰ 33 ꙰

Louisa-Margaretta had not been able to find her father or Mr Bragg. She had been sent to fetch her father, but she looked for Mr Bragg first because she no longer trusted him. Mr Bragg was not in his bedroom or in the library, and the only other haunt she knew of was the garden, where he went on his mad walks. Eventually, she found the rector in the front hall, and he looked rather distressed.

"I must beg your assistance, Miss Haddington," Mr St Clair said, all formality. "I was with our friend Mr Bragg, but I had to leave his room for but a moment, and he seems to have gone off somewhere. Perhaps you could help me find him? He was not terribly well, I am very sorry to say."

Louisa-Margaretta nearly stamped her foot. She did not wish to be cross with Judith's father, but she felt that the meeting which she had thought would help her find a murderer was turning into an unqualified disaster. The whole company had not assembled, there were threats of tedious prayers with her mama, and for all she knew, they would never get to have even a drop of tea. It was just like her mother to profess the greatest feeling for her guests while preventing them from either eating or drinking.

"I doubt we shall ever find him," she said. "But you may as well come along. This house is far too big for a single family, even when we have a thousand cousins and strangers with us."

The rector started, and she sighed. "I'm sorry?"

"Miss Haddington, I beg your pardon," he said. "You and your family have a lovely home. I am sure we shall find our friend very soon."

She felt like protesting that Mr Bragg was not her friend then thought the better of it.

They walked the halls, but they found nothing. Louisa-Margaretta dreaded having to make conversation with the rector, but he seemed to intuit her feelings and said nothing. Eventually, she found herself wishing to speak to him, an impulse that annoyed her.

"I'm sure this was not what you envisioned when my mother invited you to come and have tea with us," she said. "I am sorry that we are such poor company."

"You are excellent company for us, Miss Haddington," he said. "Especially for Judith."

"Well, her aunt does not seem to approve," Louisa-Margaretta huffed. "She did not make a secret of her feelings today, and I am surprised you got her to set foot over the threshold."

She knew she ought not to be saying such things, but a quick glance at the rector showed that he had a half smile.

"That may be true," he said, "but I have never seen my Judith leave the house so much since her mother was alive. She has not asked to wear full mourning since the night of the ball and seems to have completely forgot her mourning brooch too."

Louisa-Margaretta sniffed. "Well, I can offer an explanation for the mourning brooch, as she lost it here and I have only returned it lately. But do you not feel troubled, afraid that she should forget your late wife?"

The rector shook his head slowly. "She will not forget. But her mother would not have wished her to stay in mourning forever. She is young, and we want her to find joy and meaning. I know that is just as true for her mother as it is for me."

He said it with such perfect certainty that Louisa-Margaretta could not help but stare. She had heard people say before that loved ones are in heaven, watching every day that passes on earth, but she herself had never believed it. And here was this man, standing next to her, speaking of his wife as if she had just finished her cup of tea and gone to sit in the next room with her needlework.

It was a greater faith, she reflected, than she even had in her beloved. She felt fairly certain he was alive, but she could not know what he was doing. If his family were anything like hers, they would be marching him towards every eligible partner in their circle. She hoped that he loved her enough to resist, but each day that she failed to get word to him, she worried. If she was not quite certain of him, he might also wonder whether he really ought to rely on her. It was possible he might hear of her holiday with her bachelor cousins and expect her to marry one of them.

"How do you know?" she asked the rector.

"Beg your pardon, my child?"

"About your wife. Her wishes and what she sees from heaven. What is it that tells you?"

He paused and looked ready to answer, but a cry from the next room attracted their attention.

"Stay here, please," he said. "I shall attend to that. If it is Mr Bragg, it would not be proper to send a young lady."

❧ 34 ❧

"It would not be proper to send a young lady over to that place," said Aunt Leah, spreading marmalade on her toast with such force that the bread broke beneath it.

"Louisa-Margaretta is my friend," Judith said, and she was surprised by how truly she meant it. Somehow, her library companion had not become any less spoiled, but she had shown herself to be stronger and even a slight bit wiser than Judith had been able to see at first. "I cannot desert her."

Aunt Leah looked sternly at her other niece and her nephews, but even Miriam was not paying attention. The three eldest St Clairs had arrived back at the rectory the night before to find everyone but the servants asleep and, by mutual agreement, had not breathed a word to anyone about Mr Horace Ramsbury's death. It would be common gossip soon enough, but that was no reason to bandy it about first.

Miriam was still annoyed with her sister for leaving her out of the visit, and she was reciting the first part of "The Northern Ditty" to her brothers.

"Cold and raw the North did blow / Bleak in the morning

early / All the trees were hid with snow / Cover'd with Winter's fearly."

Judith looked sharply to see whether her sister would continue through the verses, but that was the only part their mother had ever recited to them. It was years before Judith realized that the ballad in its entirety told of a man who wished to go to bed with a young woman but was refused because he could not marry her, being already married himself.

She thought sadly of her friend. Though she had heard that some of the ladies of the upper classes were sheltered from the facts of life, still, it was not possible for Louisa-Margaretta to have been with a man without knowing that a child might result. She knew something of horses, having spent a great deal of her childhood in the countryside, and as Judith knew, even the Bible was not always perfectly vague in its allusions to these matters. Certainly, a young woman with some education ought to be at least as wary as the sharp-eyed maiden in the ballad.

But whatever her reasons, Louisa-Margaretta had been punished for them. Her condition was now not only causing trouble in her own family, it seemed to be needling Aunt Leah as well. For surely, that was one of the reasons she hoped to keep Judith from the house and from Louisa-Margaretta's influence.

"I am quite sure that she wishes to see me," said Judith again. "Perhaps I could simply have my card delivered."

"Under the circumstances, you may do no such thing," snapped her aunt. "If anyone pays a call, it will be your father."

Judith's father had not yet risen from his bed. Indeed, Judith felt the lack of sleep behind her own eyes and wondered if she might get away with seeking her bed again. But she also felt frantic and knew that even if her aunt and father allowed what they had always looked upon as the unconscionable idleness of returning to one's bed after daybreak, she would not be able to sleep.

"Then perhaps I shall go for a walk," she said, striving for brightness in her tone. "Miriam, would you like to accompany me?"

Her sister snapped to alertness. "Judith, are you mad? I should not stir out of doors in all this snow for a kingdom."

The world outside was turning white. After they arrived home the previous night, the snow must have started, and Judith realized that she had hardly glanced at a window all morning. The snow was still falling, and it was heavy. It was not weather for walking.

"I shall take care," she said. "I will not stray far from the house. But I will not remain indoors."

Louisa-Margaretta was also staring at the snow. Her eyes were dry, and she wished she could cry.

Though her removal to Derbyshire had made her sad and angry, there had been no fear in it. She was certain she would find a way to return to London eventually. But now, she truly felt like a prisoner in the large house. When they had first come, she had been well aware that she would not be able to leave easily, but now, she thought of nothing but escape. And she knew that she was not safe.

The deepest irony was that she could not show that she knew what was happening. She had to be demure, ready, unwilling to accept the idea of murder. If she gave any indication she had proof Aunt Matilda had not died by her own hand, the danger would be even greater.

And so she found herself in a circle of distressed and tearful relations an hour later. It was something like the one her mother had wished to form the night before. The difference was that Agnes and Anna were with the adults. Though she had asked her mother not to call them, Mama would have none of it.

"They'll sense things, poor lambs," she said. "They feel it keenly. And so we must have them with us. Besides, without a proper governess, they are sure to run about, sneaking biscuits and listening at keyholes."

After Mrs Haddington had delivered what seemed to be an over-long blessing, each member of the party had a chance to speak. In plain denial of the facts, they were supposed to enumerate their blessings.

Louisa-Margaretta would have said she was thankful their family circle was small, so she would not have to listen to such nonsense all morning. But Mama did not allow her to go first.

Cousin Ephraim spoke first. "I am here with my two daughters," he said. "And with all of you."

Louisa-Margaretta threw her mother a look. It was plain that Cousin Ephraim's cousins were as nothing to him when compared to his two brilliant children.

He cleared his throat. "I suppose I have few memories of Derbyshire, but it was kind of you to invite me to a village where I once spent some time, Mrs Haddington," he said. "The country is not quite as savage as I had feared."

This, apparently, was to be his only contribution. But he nagged his little Anna into speaking.

She was at an age when seeing all of the family members in the circle watching her still made her giggle and look down. "Well, I am blessed," she said, then faltered. "I have my family, and all my toys. And we will have more gifts in the new year."

"Anna," said her older sister urgently, but most of the party smiled at this.

"And I am thankful for this house, because it is pretty, and there are many fireplaces, I have counted sixteen and a half, and lots of horses, and very pretty snuff boxes for sugar," she said.

Before anyone could jump in to ask what half a fireplace could be or why she would put sugar in a snuff box, her sister had begun a rather more solemn list of blessings, one that was more refined but also less charming. "I am thankful for our family, and our good health," she said. "We are blessed to be near the church and in possession of a great many books and to be learning."

Louisa-Margaretta nearly shrugged her shoulders. If Cousin Ephraim had tried to make his firstborn in his own image, he had certainly succeeded.

Cousin Morgan's list was similarly dull, though less studied. "I am thankful to be near so many good people, both in this home and outside it," he said, turning red at the very beginning of his speech. Louisa-Margaretta wondered how long he would even be able to speak.

Not long, as it turned out. "I am thankful for my family," he said. "And that I was with family when my father . . ."

He broke off there and simply shook his head. His brother took over, his own tone resigned.

"We are thankful for all you have done for us," he said, and though he did not have a glass of wine in his hand, he had the same droll intonation of one at a party. "And thankful that at least the snow makes it an honest winter, I suppose. And that we shall soon get through Christmas and be able to forget all this, if I'm being very honest."

Mr Haddington nodded. "I am thankful for that too," he said. "And to be near family for Christmas and the new year. Wife, nephews, children. Jolly good."

It was not the most eloquent prayer, and Louisa-Margaretta easily could have pointed out that he was not properly near his own cousins or his own children (with the exception of herself), but she did not bother. She was amused that her father had used the words "jolly good" for a situation that was clearly nothing of the sort.

It was now her turn to speak, and she was silent at first. She tried to think of her blessings without reference to her separation from Isaac and without alluding to the fact that she was afraid. Someone in the circle had done a great deal of harm. Someone in their circle. Unless . . .

She gasped. "Where is Mr Bragg?"

❧ 36 ❧

Mrs Haddington's prayer circles could go on for hours, but Louisa-Margaretta's question caused quite a stir, and everyone went in search of Mr Bragg. Apparently, nobody had thought of him the night before, at least not after she and the rector abandoned their search. And in the morning, the Haddingtons had thought only of their family. Louisa-Margaretta offered to take Anna, who had clearly already made quite a map of the house and its hiding places in her head. Cousin Ephraim snapped that his daughters were to stay with him then dragged them both off by their wrists.

Louisa-Margaretta's father took her aside. "Look, Lou," he said, using the name for her that she had begged him to stop using for years. "It's nice, isn't it, that Anna and Agnes are sisters? They are quite different, of course."

She gave a deep sigh. She did not feel particularly kindly disposed towards any of her brothers at the moment, seeing as none of them had bothered to come to Derbyshire. She knew they all had their reasons, but she decided that a sister would have been even more cold and distant in her condemnation of Louisa-Margaretta's actions. What was the point of having any siblings if they all turned to cowards at the first hint of trouble?

"I suppose it's rather sweet, the little pair of them," she said without meaning it. "Didn't Mr Bragg ever come back last night?"

"Don't think any of us looked for him, Lou," was the reply. "I thought he might as well go off on his own."

She grimaced. "Well, he might be anywhere in the house. You'll help me look, Papa?"

"Yes, Lou."

They began walking the halls in silence.

When they came upon the housekeeper, she gave an apologetic nod. "I'm afraid some of his things are missing," she said. "And it sounds very much like he was one of the men to leave from the village yesterday."

"How can they go in such weather?" said Louisa-Margaretta, marvelling. "I wouldn't think anyone would be leaving in the snow."

"Northern horses, miss," said their housekeeper. "There are very few days of the year when nobody can get through."

Louisa-Margaretta found herself unclenching her fists. She had wondered whether she might find Mr Bragg's body tucked away somewhere, or worse, a living and murderous Mr Bragg. But it appeared that she had got it all wrong. He was gone, and for good with any luck. They did not need to find him nor to condemn him for what he had done.

Another young lady would have looked out at the sun on the snow and wondered what her duty was to the world at large. She would have thought about whether to make public Mr Bragg's horrific actions, even at great cost to the family. For Louisa-Margaretta was sure that the man was behind not one but two murders and that no suicides had taken place within her home.

But she had never been civic-minded, and the man's desertion only made her thankful to have a day to herself before the Christmas festivities began again.

"I'll go and find Agnes and Anna," she said. As a rule, she was not interested in providing Christmas cheer for children, but she felt that she did owe some sort of penance for the efficacy with which God, or perhaps some kindly Christmas sprite, had dispatched Mr Bragg. "Perhaps I can give them paper and we can make a start on the ornaments for tomorrow."

"Very well, Lou," said her father. "But I did wish to speak to you about something."

She was down the hall, hardly listening to him. The snow was thick outside, and she was in search of anything that might help her feel festive, her heart light with the knowledge that now she could think only of her love and not of death.

While she was thinking about her new mission, she passed the part of the second floor where she could see the front door. She had a vague sense that somebody was being turned away from the front door, but she did not spare even a moment to see who had arrived or why that person was not going to stay.

It was night before Louisa-Margaretta finally worked it out. Mr Bragg as the murderer? Her aunt had been expecting Mr Bragg, that much was certain. Louisa-Margaretta realized, with some regret, that Aunt Matilda might have felt just as hemmed in by the conventions of the ball as she had. So she arranged a little time away with a friend, in a room she knew would almost certainly be abandoned. And because she did not turn immediately to face the door, she thought at first that it was Mr Bragg who had arrived.

But their interaction did not make sense. Mr Bragg would not have brought her cake and then left. He would certainly have stayed. If they were both trying to escape the ball, then they would have lingered over the cake. Someone else had come with the cake then quickly departed, leaving only the death sentence of a poisoned slice.

When Judith and Louisa-Margaretta ran into Mr Bragg, or when he staggered into them, he was near the ballroom. He had probably meant to go up to the library to meet with Aunt Matilda but lost his nerve once he realized he was discovered. In fact, Louisa-Margaretta remembered, he had seemed rather flustered. Had he run up to the library after seeing them, gone back down the stairs, then reached the ballroom before the two much younger ladies? Certainly not. It would have been difficult or even impossible because of the trouble he had with his knees. It was the reason, in fact, that he didn't do any dancing. When he had his sticks, he could walk creditably well, and that was what he had used when shooting and during his mad bouts of pacing. But it would have looked strange for him to use them during the ball. He was a proud man. And apart from that, stairs were exceedingly difficult for him. She had only ever seen him take them slowly.

She was not absolutely sure why he was in so much fear of being discovered, but she reasoned that his behaviour was ruder than her aunt's. For a member of a family to escape a ball was permissible, as she herself knew. In a guest, a Mr Bragg or a Miss St Clair, such a transgression might not be so easily forgiven.

She wondered if Judith had worked it out. And thinking of how she had been happy only hours earlier, sitting near the fire at a table with her Cousin Ephraim's daughters and a mess of paper and other decorations, Louisa-Margaretta felt a new chill. She had left herself vulnerable, and perhaps the killer might yet be ready to strike.

She hid under the bedclothes, wondering how many hours there were until morning.

She could not pretend that her vigilance would be enough to keep her family safe. She needed Judith.

$\mathscr{H}$ 38 $\mathscr{H}$

"Judith, you are needed in the vestry today," said Aunt Leah with a stern look.

Judith did not know what she had done to deserve scorn at such an early hour. Her arguments with her aunt, conducted in the early morning over a meagre breakfast, were becoming a daily occurrence.

"I believe everything is ready," she said.

"Someone has been trying to get in again," said her aunt. "They very nearly broke a window. But one of the Carrothers boys heard them, and whoever it was ran away. We must make certain they did not get in and steal anything."

"I am sure that whatever silver is left would be more than enough for a humble manger," said Judith. "In fact, so long as we have a bit of straw, we need little else. After all, Father does not approve of excessive celebration for Christmas, especially not in his church."

"And I do not approve of theft," said her aunt. "Imagine if the church were to lose some of its most valuable items in his first month as rector. His reputation would be irreparably damaged."

"Any reputation can be repaired," Judith said, though she did not particularly believe it. It was one of her greatest worries for Louisa-Margaretta, though certainly not the greatest one.

She had been told that her friend would not see her yesterday, and yet she had cause to believe that they had not yet protected themselves from the reach of a killer. But the Haddingtons were a very grand family, and that would make it more difficult for her to reason with her friend. She knew very well, as Aunt Leah said, that her father's position was both excellent and tenuous. She could not afford to make an enemy, but neither could she afford to lose her friend.

There was a knock that startled even Aunt Leah. Judith realized with great relief that she would not have to solve the problem of not seeing Louisa-Margaretta. Aunt Leah followed Judith to the front door, where Sally was taking Louisa-Margaretta's coat.

"Good morning," said Louisa-Margaretta, her hair covered in snow. "I wish you both a very happy Christmas Eve."

Judith blinked. "And to you as well, Miss Haddington."

She and her aunt stood near the door. They should have invited Louisa-Margaretta to the parlor immediately, but both were surprised by her arrival. They knew full well that they were the only members of the family currently awake, and they might have to warn the others not to venture downstairs before they were dressed.

"Do come and join us in the parlor, Miss Haddington," said Judith. "Perhaps you would like some breakfast?"

She had been using Louisa-Margaretta's mouthful of a Christian name for some time. But the shock of seeing her there early on the snowy morning had forced her into a more deferential form of address.

She had offered breakfast without thinking. Aunt Leah had grown up being expected to help in the kitchen, as the family had not been able to afford a cook. Judith, though brought up in slightly easier circumstances, also knew how to cook. It would have been no trouble for them to lay the table and toast the bread themselves. But it seemed a poor spread to offer a guest.

"No, thank you for your kindness," said Louisa-Margaretta with a forced smile. Judith looked down at her friend's hands and saw that they were trembling.

Louisa-Margaretta, seeing Judith's gaze, quickly hid her hands in her cloak.

"I was hoping to take a turn with my friend," she said, "before we all gather later for the service. Miss St Clair, if you would accompany me? I brought a horse for you, of course, so you will not have to walk."

"I sh-should be happy to," said Judith without looking at her aunt. "Only, it seems that the walk will be rather cold, so let me prepare."

"Of course," said Louisa-Margaretta, not pointing out that it was also quite cold at the entrance to the home, where her half-frozen garments were beginning to drip on the hard floor. Though there had been even more snow on Louisa-Margaretta's coat, there seemed to be plenty on her dress and petticoat as well.

"If you will excuse us," said Aunt Leah, and accompanied Judith up to her bedroom.

"Judith," she said, holding fast to the only decently warm cloak that her niece owned, "I beg you not to go with that impossible person."

Judith glared. She could not grab the cloak without revealing the package she held in her own hands, covered by a lesser cloak. And it would be too dangerous for Aunt Leah to know what she carried, just as it would be dangerous if Judith did not take what she had discovered to Wycliff Castle immediately. "It is perfectly respectable, Aunt Leah," she said. "And indeed, father's position may be —"

"Your father's position is not dependent on you indulging every whim of a spoiled young lady," she replied. "There is something very wrong in that household, and you should keep well away. If not for your own sake, think of the rest of the family."

"Is that what I should think of, then?" asked Judith. "Only my own family?"

Clutching her package under the cloak, she thought of Louisa-Margaretta's position. Who knew what dangers might be posed to a woman who expected her lying-in to take place in the new year, riding on horseback through the snow? Judith had been used to seeing ladies even in the early days of that condition rest, faint, and even avoid company if they wished it. But her friend had ridden through the snow for her help.

"I am thinking of my friend," she said crossly, even though she was angry with Louisa-Margaretta for rejecting her help one day then begging for it the morning of the next. "And you heard what she said — there is a horse for me. I will only go up the lane with her, and I won't be gone long."

It wasn't exactly a falsehood. After all, some would consider Wycliff Castle only up the lane, and Judith was fairly certain that this would be their destination.

Aunt Leah frowned. "And there is no way of stopping you?"

"None," said Judith.

Aunt Leah only shook her head. "My child," she said, "I do not recognize you. When you come home, you must speak with your father. But I will not stop you now, because he has a hard day's work ahead of him, and I would very much like him to rest."

$\maltese$ 39 $\maltese$

Once Judith was on her horse, she realized how cold the day was. It was even crueller than she had expected. The wind whipped the snow into her face, and she immediately fell behind Louisa-Margaretta, even at a walk. There was too much snow for her to know her surroundings, and she feared that if her horse could not find the way back to the stable, she would be lost in the woods. She worried that the sensible advice she had always followed as a child — the directive to find water and follow it downhill — would not save her life if everything was frozen.

"Slow down!" she hissed. "Not everyone is an accomplished rider."

"There is no time," insisted Louisa-Margaretta. "Mr Bragg did not poison my aunt and uncle, and now, he is gone. He may have fled in fear."

"Well, of course he did not poison them!" said Judith. "What reason would he have for poisoning either of them? He is not even part of the family."

"But he may have been working with the poisoner," said Louisa-Margaretta. "Else why would he run away? I thought of that last night, but it was too late to speak with you. If only Mama hadn't kept us praying half the day. I needed to speak with you, Judith!"

"Then why did you turn me away?" Judith asked. "I could easily have enlightened you! Of course there is a poisoner at work in the home." Her fingers felt even colder at the thought, remembering her chilly walk home and the depth of Aunt Leah's disappointment.

Louisa-Margaretta frowned. "I never turned you away," she said. "When?"

"When I came to visit yesterday," she said. "You said that you would not see me."

"Now you are the one who is lying!" insisted Louisa-Margaretta, unconsciously spurring her horse on until she was trotting at a pace dangerous in the snow, one Judith could hardly match. She held the reins tighter.

"I am not lying," said Judith slowly. "Only, I did not speak to you. It is what I was told."

At this, Louisa-Margaretta managed to rein in the grey, blinking steadily over at her friend. "Who told you," she said. "Who told you that I did not wish to see you, when I wanted nothing else?"

Judith thought only a moment before giving Louisa-Margaretta a name. After she spoke, neither of them needed more than a moment to realise the significance of Judith's story.

They hurried to Wycliff Castle, no longer bothering about the snow and the cold.

❧ 40 ❧

The grand house was not warm, but it was filled with activity. Mrs Haddington had insisted on starting the decorations, even though half the boughs they brought in were soaked with snow and had to be left to dry on cloths near the fires (but not too near) until they were fit to be used on the walls.

"My dear," said Mrs Haddington to Judith. "Have you come to help, and in all this snow, too? You are truly a blessing for our family and our dear Louisa-Margaretta in particular."

Judith felt embarrassed at this allusion to her friend's delicate condition. "Yes, well," she said. "I thought that perhaps it might be helpful to have another pair of hands, as the house is so very large, and the weather has been foul."

She wondered why Mrs Haddington had not taken more care instead of allowing Louisa-Margaretta to go out. Perhaps she no longer had even the faintest hope of controlling her daughter.

"You are a blessing to us all," said Mrs Haddington, her smile warm. "Here, Louisa-Margaretta, dearest! All the things we should have brought from the woods are drying, but Cook could spare some of the rosemary. And here is a basket of holly that is dry, or nearly. Perhaps you could take your friend back to the music room. I daresay that is where we will spend a great deal of time, as Anna and Agnes have been longing for music."

"Thank you," said Judith as Louisa-Margaretta took one of the baskets and passed the other to her. When they left the room, she was not sure at first whether they were headed to the music room, perhaps by way of some shortcut. But when they went down a passageway that was not familiar to her, she knew that her friend had another aim.

"What are you doing?" she murmured. "Your mother will know that we have not decorated."

"We can decorate after," said Louisa-Margaretta, stopping by a closed door. "This is Mr Bragg's room. We must find out why he left."

"I'm not sure his room will be able to tell us that," said Judith, looking over her shoulder as she wondered how they could possibly explain their presence.

"It will tell us something," said Louisa-Margaretta, opening the door and hastily beckoning Judith to step through the doorway. She closed the door behind them.

Whoever had cleaned the room had done so efficiently. Not even the linens were left. The grate was quite tidy, and if Mr Bragg had left any possessions, they did not remain in the room. The floor had been swept, and the windows were clean. With no fire, the room was cold, and Judith realized that she could see her breath.

"This is odd," said Louisa-Margaretta. "This wall, here."

Judith had also noticed a place that seemed uneven. It was as if the wall had not been put in properly.

She went over and tried it. There was a door that opened to the next room.

"It's only a door," she said. "One of the owners must have decided that it did not suit their taste, but instead of getting rid of it, they simply covered it."

Louisa-Margaretta was frowning, gazing into the larger room Judith had revealed. "That is my Aunt Matilda's room," she said.

Judith thought about correcting her, since Aunt Matilda had not inhabited that room for some time, but instead, she followed her friend through.

Louisa-Margaretta sat in the chair at the dressing table, looking in the mirror. "I suppose she used this mirror," she said. "Is it not strange to think that we are all to die one day? That there is nothing separating us from the dead but a matter of months or years? Arithmetic, that's all it is. Of course, I have always loathed arithmetic."

Judith, who had been contemplating the nature of death constantly since her mother fell ill, made no answer. This thought and a thousand others had already occurred to her. And the fact that she had always loved arithmetic was of little comfort. Instead, she walked about the room.

Something about it was not right. It was just as tidy as the other, if more feminine in its decor. Then she realized. The door on this side had also been hidden, and a piece of paper had fallen out when they opened it.

She opened the letter. It had once been sealed but now was only folded. Clearly, it had been read, either by the intended recipient or by someone else.

My beloved, I wish to give you all my love. Though this holiday is more trying than some, I rejoice in our proximity and in the kindness that has enabled it. Do not despair. For the rest of my life, every waking moment that I can decently manage, I shall spend with you. All my love.

The hand was very elegant. She believed it to be a man's. Wordlessly, she passed it to Louisa-Margaretta, who read it and immediately started to sob, slouching over the dressing table.

At first, it seemed a strange response to a letter written by a stranger. The sentiments could have nothing to do with Louisa-Margaretta.

Then, remembering too late that Louisa-Margaretta had experienced the most consequential kind of heartbreak, something far worse than being simply crossed in love, Judith touched her friend's shoulder.

"I'm sorry!" she said. "I'm sorry! Still, I think it may help give an explanation."

Her friend was still sobbing, but she found a handkerchief and raked it across her eyes with anger. "Oh, it explains nothing, only that people have always been miserable."

"Well," said Judith gently, "it sounds as if Mr Bragg was not exactly miserable."

Now Louisa-Margaretta nearly stopped crying. "Mr Bragg?" she said, her voice coming out as a croak. "What has he to do with any of this?"

Judith started. "Well, as the author of that letter. You know."

She could manage to say no more. She was not usually one to tell even mildly bawdy jokes in company, and she had not expected that she would need to spell out the meaning of the letter to a friend who was much more experienced in these matters.

"Mr Bragg did not write this note," said Louisa-Margaretta. "He is married, did we never tell you? He was the only man in this house, besides my father, of course, who was not being cajoled into courting me."

"It seems as though he did not think of you," said Judith quietly. "He thought only of your aunt."

＊ 41 ＊

Louisa-Margaretta stormed out of the room, Judith
hot on her heels.

"I do not know how you could say such a thing
about my aunt," she raved. "And you a rector's daughter!
Speaking ill of the dead!"

"I do not mean to speak ill," said Judith hastily. "Truly, I
do not. But it would explain —"

"It is nonsense," hissed Louisa-Margaretta. "And it is a
filthy accusation."

Judith began to grow impatient. Louisa-Margaretta had
not only seen the letter and the secret doors but also Mr
Bragg's wild and genuine grief. And Louisa-Margaretta herself
obviously knew something about "friendship" between a man
and a woman requiring subterfuge in certain circumstances
and the consequences when such a romance was discovered.
It was silly of her to pretend to be absolutely innocent, especially considering her condition.

"It is not an accusation, it is a conclusion based on what
we know to be true and the parts of this murder that were
not explained," said Judith, grown haughty. "If you do not

wish to believe it, you may go to your mother and ask for her views on the matter."

Louisa-Margaretta, handkerchief now bunched in her palm, her eyes red from crying, let out a little laugh. "If you knew anything about my mother, anything at all, you would realize that this could not possibly happen under her roof. Why, she is more devout than anyone I have ever met, with the possible exception of your father!"

Judith felt the compliment, though she knew her friend had not meant to give it. She herself had long been proud that her papa was devoted to his faith, where in his profession, she had seen so much hypocrisy. Indeed, this time of year often provided the sorriest of examples. Every year, her father complained about members of the clergy eating, drinking, and gambling without any reflection on the significance of Christmas or the struggles of their parishioners. Mrs Haddington, with her insistence on prayer and propriety, seemed similar in certain ways, though her loud voice and tendency to embrace everyone was certainly a contrast with the rector's quiet nature.

"Ask her, then," said Judith. "And I will go and decorate the music room."

"Fine," said Louisa-Margaretta, glaring at her friend. "But I know exactly what she is going to say."

"Of course, my dear," said Louisa-Margaretta's mother. "I did not wish you to know. But yes, I knew about Mr Bragg and your aunt. As the hostess, I must have known, must I not? An invitation to a man outside our family party, one who might be inclined to gossip, was not something I could afford to take lightly."

They were sitting in Louisa-Margaretta's bedroom. She had insisted that her mother accompany her to that private chamber so she might ask about the strange letter. Judith had acted as if she were about one hundred years old, inured to the scandal implied by that missive, but Louisa-Margaretta could not believe it.

But Mama was rather too direct in her response. Louisa-Margaretta could feel the slight. She was one source of shame to her family, the reason her parents had been forced to buy a large new home in the faraway mountains to get her married off as quickly as they possibly could, in order that she might keep her admittance to polite society.

The only outsider who could be trusted to keep quiet

about these plans was one who had a great deal to lose himself. In even issuing the invitation, putting Mr Bragg in a position to learn exactly what was happening within the old walls of Wycliff Castle, the genteel Mrs Haddington had nearly made herself into a blackmailer.

"So my aunt and Mr Bragg are simply allowed to sin, is that it?" she said tartly. "Whereas I must forsake my love and marry another? That is a fine sort of hypocrisy."

Her mother sighed. "For your aunt, she was past the age where that sort of thing would be much talked about. Even if it did get out, it would not be considered a scandal. Mr Bragg may have a wife, but in many ways, that makes the whole thing rather easier for society. And there is the matter of their ages, which is no small consideration."

"I was not aware that the expectation of virtue was limited to a certain set," said Louisa-Margaretta, her voice icy. "Mother, how could you?"

Her mother smoothed the place next to her on the bedclothes. Louisa-Margaretta refused to sit but, out of habit, came to stand next to her mother.

"My dear," said Mama. "You know very little of marriage." She held up a hand over her daughter's protest and continued. "We see all sorts of marriages, especially in our set. Some that are based on mutual understanding and others that are purely mercenary. The origin is not necessarily the best indicator of how the husband and wife will get on, especially when it is a matter of decades."

Louisa-Margaretta scowled. "Yours was a love marriage," she said. "And it seems to be going rather well, considering that you and Papa are happily conspiring against me."

"If we are conspiring, my dear, it is only for your benefit. You must believe that."

When Louisa-Margaretta was silent, her mother went on.

"Some of the marriages," she said delicately, "are not bad ones. But if one of the parties wishes to spend time with another and that can be arranged without scandal, that may well be to the benefit of all."

"Even if it is a sin? Nothing good can come from an individual ignoring his conscience and choosing to sin. At least, that is what I have been told."

Her mother shifted. "I am not condoning it, exactly," she said. "But your aunt had no money and very little privacy. She went from one relative to another for her entire life. And so if there were any friend with whom she wished to spend time, there was always some difficulty about her living situation. I thought, at her request, that we might spare her this particular burden, if only for a fortnight."

Louisa-Margaretta recalled her aunt's efforts. "But she was making such trouble about marrying me off! It seemed her only aim."

"I cannot say whether your aunt would have been happier if she married, dear," said her mama. "But it is possible that she might have been more independent. And I am sure that is something she would have prized highly."

Louisa-Margaretta sighed, remembering her aunt's consumption of wine, her stories about Gretna Green and the weddings "over the anvil" that were real weddings all the same. The stories had seemed to contain some kind of bitterness. She understood it now.

She also remembered how her aunt had talked about legitimate children and the reasons that people came to Gretna Green. She looked at her mother and did not want to ask but could not help herself.

"Did Aunt Matilda ever have a child?" she asked.

Mama started. "Why would you think that?"

"Well, she kept saying that a child whose parents were

married at the time of the birth was the child of both parents, no matter how late the marriage. It was a very common reason that people came to Gretna Green, she said."

At this, Louisa-Margaretta could not look at her mother, but she waited eagerly for the answer.

"She did not have a child herself," said her mother. "But she understood the benefits of legitimacy. She also understood that a parent, if they were not recognized by the law, might wish to do things for their own child."

Louisa-Margaretta's eyes narrowed. "The sort of parent who abandons their child? Who is cold and unfeeling but attempts to send money later? I am very glad my aunt is not that sort of person. I might hate her if she were."

She was surprised to see tears come to her mother's eyes. "I know you do not truly mean that, my dear," she said. "God forgives all of us, sinners though we are, and He asks that we extend that same forgiveness to each other."

Seeing that Louisa-Margaretta was not listening, having fallen back into her habit of ignoring these little sermons, she added, "Also, it is possible for a natural parent to let their child grow up with individuals who are better placed to care for them. And it is possible for them not to know they have had a child if they are a man."

This answer irritated Louisa-Margaretta even more. It seemed to her as if men got away with all sorts of things, while ladies like her aunt, who she had always considered the epitome of freedom in her spinsterhood, were allowed to do very little. But she was relieved that her aunt did not leave behind any children, only a lover.

Another realization came to her. "Mr Bragg," she said. "He was not really mad, was he?"

Her mother shook her head. "Not mad, dear, only grieving. That is why we all wished to be kind to him. But it is not easy to grieve a great love amongst strangers, and I expect eventually, it all became too much for him."

Louisa-Margaretta, who suspected that there were other reasons for the gentleman's departure, stood up. "I've left Miss St Clair to decorate all alone," she said. "She will be expecting me."

❧ 43 ☙

Judith, in fact, was not expecting Louisa-Margaretta. As she decorated in the music room, she had been looking about and admiring the instruments. Although her heart still raced from the argument with her friend, she knew that she had interpreted the letter quite accurately. It was the only sensible explanation for Mr Bragg's presence in the family party. He had not come with the intention of poisoning anyone, and after his only reason for joining was gone, he left. He, more than anyone else, would have understood his sweetheart well enough to know that she had no plans to take her own life. Therefore, he must have been painfully aware that there was a killer on the loose.

Still, they had not been able to get any sense of what Mr Bragg knew or suspected. If he had abandoned them, did he feel that the danger was over, or was he a coward running away from it?

She reflected on the two deaths. There was a penniless aunt, a spinster like herself, who had apparently been spending her nights with a married man. Judith was far less shocked than Louisa-Margaretta. Such arrangements were less alien to her, she supposed. Most people assumed that as a rector's daughter, she was brought up without any knowledge of how the world outside the church walls turned. In fact, given her father's duty to his parishioners and the great number of times that he or her mother were needed during some sort of crisis, Judith was not at all unfamiliar with the fickle nature of the human heart.

At the cold window, she offered up a small prayer for Mr Bragg's safety. Her father had told her that Mr Bragg felt himself under threat. He, like nearly everyone else, had believed this to be a false tale that grief was telling the poor man. But Judith realized with a chill that Mr Bragg's interpretation was entirely accurate. He may have even witnessed the second murder, though she hoped he had got away before it. He would have had more knowledge of the killer's habits than she, and it was possible that he had tried to intervene. She and Louisa-Margaretta had taken his departure as a sign of guilt, but in truth, they could not be sure that he was alive. She hoped he had managed to make his way out of Derbyshire before the killer realized what he knew and decided to take his life. Perhaps Mr Bragg had not been faithful to his family, but he deserved a chance to make amends.

Judith thought about the last time she was in the music room and what had felt like an interminable wait for tea. Although the tea set had been very fine indeed, she had been overcome by a sense of unease, as if she had known then that Mr Horace Ramsbury was also being poisoned, even as they sat there.

The memory of all of it came back to her. The fine tea service. The way that nobody had been in the room with her and Aunt Leah, other than Louisa-Margaretta and her cousin Mr Morgan Ramsbury. And then Mrs Haddington finally came in, but both of them were sent away, and it was ages before the company assembled. Mr Bragg had not been the only one missing.

It came to her then. The strange nature of that gathering was not only owing to Mrs Haddington's late arrival and Mr Bragg's absence. There was another person whose behavior was decidedly strange, only Judith had been thinking so much about the Haddington family that she had hardly noticed.

With a start, she darted out of the music room, leaving the decorations there, and ran to the schoolroom.

❧ 44 ❧

Louisa-Margaretta, who met her friend in the passage, found her arm gripped tightly as Judith took her to the music room and forced her to sit down by the pianoforte.

"Really," Louisa-Margaretta said. "There can be no cause —"

"Listen," hissed Judith. "I've found the poison."

Louisa-Margaretta stared. "Where?"

Judith's eyes flickered over to the door. "I'll tell you. But for heaven's sake, keep your voice down. I don't want any interruptions. I already put up some of the decorations, and there is no time to finish the task now."

Taking in the room, Louisa-Margaretta saw that the decorating did not look like Judith's work at all. While her friend was habitually tidy, sprigs of rosemary and holly were stuck in various corners with no apparent system or reason. That in itself might well give them away, but she hoped that nobody would take notice. Perhaps she could say it was her own work, though she loathed decorating and felt sure her lie would be discovered.

"It was what Anna said about the snuff boxes having sugar in them," said Judith. "At first, I thought the girls might have taken a snuff box and used it as a sugar bowl or pretended to. But then I realized that the case where they are kept would be a good place to hide arsenic, though I don't know who has the keys."

"You don't have a key," said Louisa-Margaretta. "How did you know it was arsenic?"

Judith shook her head, impatient. "I can see through the glass that it doesn't look a bit like sugar. Besides, there is only one of them that has the powder. It is the one with King George's portrait."

Louisa-Margaretta shook her head. Judith, privately, had thought that a snuff box with a portrait of the mad king was not the worst place to hide poison. After all, there were many who suspected that the king himself had been poisoned. It was one of many explanations for the root of his madness. Judith herself, having seen many people lose their wits, was not particularly fond of this theory.

"We still don't have proof of murder," said Louisa-Margaretta. "We could tell Mama and Papa, and they might just say it was . . . well, that my aunt and uncle took their own lives, in both cases. After all, Uncle Horace was very ill, and we don't know how long he would have lived. And I am sure there is arsenic somewhere here. Even I know that it is effective against rats."

"We don't need proof," said Judith, flushing in anger. "If we do nothing —"

Mr Morgan Ramsbury entered the room and smiled at both of them. "How are you?" he said. "I have been sent to tell you that lunch will be served shortly." He surveyed the room — the hasty decorations, the two silent young women. "What are you doing here?"

It was Louisa-Margaretta who was quick with an answer,

sitting herself down at the harp and playing an old tune. "We are practicing," she said as she stared at Judith, willing her to sing. "We are going to sing for the company later."

Mr Ramsbury's smile went from friendly, if reserved, to puzzled as he studied both of them. One was playing, neither was singing, and Judith feared that if they did not come up with a better reason, they would give themselves away before they had a chance to come up with a plan to seek justice for her friend's murdered relatives.

Louisa-Margaretta began to sing. "Oh, Christmas Day is here, Oh, Christmas Day is here, Lots of boughs and holly bring, and tidings of good cheer, Christmas Day is here, oh, Christmas Day is here."

She finished with a flourish, and Judith was relieved. She could never have invented such a thing in no time at all. And in Mr Morgan Ramsbury's presence, she felt that it was nearly impossible to speak.

"I have never heard those words before," he said, coming over. "Are they new?"

"Yes," said Judith, blushing. "Very new. We will be down to lunch shortly."

Mama was the only reasonable choice. The two of them had agreed that if they could not get both Louisa-Margaretta's parents and tell them together, they would start with Mama. She was less likely to dismiss what they were saying, although Judith had some concerns that religious forgiveness would get in the way of any type of intervention in the matter.

When they found her, she was in the kitchens, giving some late instructions for the luncheon. It was impossible to be truly out of hearing of the servants, so they waited until she was finished and then went upstairs with her to the dining room, which was still empty. Louisa-Margaretta reasoned that the house was so large it would take Cousin Morgan ages to find everyone and summon them.

"Mama," she said. "My aunt and uncle did not die by their own hand."

"Oh, sweetheart," she said, and the depth of her reaction showed Louisa-Margaretta that she had thought of this possibility herself. "Surely, you cannot be serious, and to say such slanderous words in front of our guest! Miss St Clair, you must forgive us."

"I assure you, Mrs Haddington," said Judith, "I am in agreement with your daughter."

Mama did not laugh at them, to her credit, but she did shake her head firmly. "Then you are both very ill-informed. I'll not hear such talk again."

"But Mama," said Louisa-Margaretta. "We cannot spend Christmas Eve entertaining a murderer —"

"How can you say such a thing?" said her mother. "Take your place, and quickly. Once everyone is assembled, we must eat at once. We are already behind in our preparations for the holiday."

Louisa-Margaretta did not take her place, but she had run out of arguments. She knew that the only course still open to her was to confess what she and Judith had done. But it was important not to let everyone hear.

"Both Miss St Clair and I were in the library," she said quietly, "on the night that Aunt Matilda died. We know that she did not get the slice of cake herself. It was brought to her."

Her mother, who had been straightening one of the soup spoons, paused. "Then it was a generous gift," she said. "And if your aunt added something to it later, something that proved fatal, then it was a moment of madness. And may God forgive her that moment. That is all there is to say on the matter."

Judith had never contradicted Mrs Haddington before, and she did not appear inclined to do so at present. She was casting nervous glances at the door.

"Girls, girls, our guests will be here at any minute," said Mrs Haddington, putting her hands on both young ladies and steering them to the door. "I am sure that both of these unexpected deaths have been quite hard on you, but really, to speak of murder is simply unacceptable. I will not have it."

Judith, who had been allowing herself to be directed, now stood firm.

"Louisa-Margaretta was almost killed as well," she said. "It was during the shooting party. Someone shot at her, and they might have killed her."

"I'm sure it was an accident," said Mama, although her voice faltered a bit. Hearing such an accusation from the meek Miss St Clair rather than her own daughter must have thrown her.

"It was not an accident," said Louisa-Margaretta firmly. "Where I was standing, there were no birds. The man who fired on me was shooting towards rock, at the side of the mountain. And it was because I had gone up there, on my own, ahead of the party."

"Which is why you were so upset that day," said Mrs Haddington. "When you finally came home, you were frantic."

"Yes," said Louisa-Margaretta. "And it was because Judith and I already knew that our aunt had been killed. And though we tried to prevent a second death, we could not."

Mrs Haddington held the back of a chair. "I see. And who do you believe the poisoner to have been?"

There was a commotion outside the door and the sound of rapid footsteps.

"Get him," cried Judith. "Louisa-Margaretta, quickly, we must go after him!"

※　46　※

By the time they got out the door, Louisa-Margaretta knew what they had to do. There must have been a horse nearby, for he had taken off quickly on horseback, though she hoped that riding without any tack would slow him down. The bay he was riding was of tolerable size and speed, but even an excellent rider would have a difficult time without a saddle when the ground was frozen. Though, of course, there would be the greater warmth that the horse's back itself would provide. She had been surprised that even in Derbyshire winter, the horses spent a great deal of time out of doors, living in the sheltered stables only during the night and the very worst storms, but she was thankful that any horse she chose would be able to run through the cold fields with no trouble.

Louisa-Margaretta raced toward the stables. With so many years riding sidesaddle, she knew she could not simply ride a horse with no saddle at all and keep any sort of speed. Judith was fast enough calling for the grey mare, and Louisa-Margaretta took her friend's shawl as two shivering young grooms raced out. The mare had been nicknamed

Godiva due to her temper, but Louisa-Margaretta was thankful that the man she was pursuing had left the fastest horse behind.

He had gone on the path, at least at first, and that was where she tried to follow. They none of them knew the area well, at least not yet, but Louisa-Margaretta had done enough riding to give her some sense of how she ought to go. All the excitement and terror of the hunt rose within her.

Judith had also asked for a horse but must have been far too slow. She did not sense her friend behind her. But she rode on, determined to find the other rider.

It still snowed, but there was no wind, and the flakes fell softly as if obedient to the urgent nature of her quest. Louisa-Margaretta began to feel angry at herself. She should not have let him know, should have made sure nobody was near the room when she was telling her mother.

But there had been no time.

Judith probably would have found the path up the mountain to be too steep and treacherous. Even Louisa-Margaretta, her bare hands freezing as she buried them tightly in Godiva's rough mane, wondered about the reasoning of the people who designed and built the road, thinking them simple to force a path up such a steep hillside. Perhaps a very small wagon might pass, but only after getting stuck several times. Indeed, it was likely a better road for pleasure seekers wishing to have a summer picnic than for laborers, farmers, or hunters.

But her horse was strong and did not tire. She gave thanks again for her saddle, because she began to see the other rider. He was nearly at the middle of the hill, she saw, but she expected to overtake him in no time.

And then he turned and began to ride through the woods, across the steep hillside.

Louisa-Margaretta had no choice but to follow. If he was

off the path, she could not know where he was going unless she followed him.

She could see her breath before her. In a sense, the riding itself was easier, because even hot-blooded Godiva had to slow to get over the rough ground. But now, the horses were more evenly matched, both having to make their way through the forest, and he was gaining no longer.

Her hands, meanwhile, were red, and her breath was coming in ragged gasps. She wondered if the evil man's aim was not to tire the horse but to tire the rider, because she was wishing she had managed to eat more and wondering if she might stop Godiva so she could have a drink of water.

The large horse slowed as they entered a thicket of trees, and she grabbed a clump of snow, forcing it into her mouth and gasping as the cold water ran down her throat.

That was all she could manage. There was no more time.

With trepidation, she noticed that they were near a stream. The ice was frozen, but she knew it would not be enough to hold a horse.

If they followed the stream, they would reach a lake, one that came close to the village. Anyone who did not cross the stream would be forced to ride where there were many more people, dogs, and perhaps carriages. And there was no bridge, not for miles.

It had been years since Louisa-Margaretta had been a daring jumper. In fact, when she broke her leg after a jump, it had nearly been enough to put her off riding entirely. If not for her brother Loftus, she might well have never got back into the saddle. She had never repaid him for all those gentle walks around the gardens on fat ponies, the only way she could ride for a whole summer without crying and nearly falling out of the saddle from fright. Her whole family had been shocked, since Louisa-Margaretta was a fearless person by nature, but the ordeal had been so horrid that even she had been terrified by the memory.

Gradually, she had recovered her seat, and she was soon ready to jump over walls on hunts easily enough. But a wide and frozen creek was a different thing. Quite apart from her fear for herself, there was Godiva to think of, who could be killed by a clumsy jump.

She recalled that her aunt and uncle had already been killed. Two people who were loved by their families in spite of their tempers, in spite of their penchant for keeping secrets that had the power to do very great harm.

The woods were thinning. They neared the lake. She rode the wrong way to let him think her defeated.

And then he managed to jump the creek on the bay, even without a saddle.

Any hesitation Louisa-Margaretta had been holding deserted her. Her heart was floating as she and the grey horse moved as one, cantering to the creek before jumping over it easily. The landing was not a soft one, but it was safe enough, and soon, they were in a farmer's field.

Open ground. Once more, she was gaining.

But instead of heading wide, she saw that the bay was going around the lake, and again, she wondered if it was just an effort to tire her own horse. If it was, it was in vain. Godiva was sweating, breathing heavily, but Louisa-Margaretta knew full well that her endurance was not likely to fail. Even as they approached the village then drew closer to her home once again, entering the very grounds, she was puzzled.

Could he be leading her on a chase, hoping simply to lose her, or to reenter her parents' house and tell everyone that he was mad?

No. He had a very different aim, and Louisa-Margaretta only guessed it when it was far too late to stop him.

She followed Cousin Theo into the church, only to stare as he opened the door to the room where the records were kept. He had the door open just a crack when he saw her. "Stop," she said, running after him. "Stop!"

He turned towards her with a sneer, leaving the door to the vestry slightly ajar. "Little Louisa-Margaretta. I told your friend what a fine horsewoman you are, and I was correct. But you were not quick enough to keep me from getting what I came for, so I must beg you to move aside."

Louisa-Margaretta folded her arms in front of her. "I shall not move one inch," she insisted. "You are to turn yourself in at once and confess your crimes, may God have mercy on your soul."

"I do not expect God to have any mercy on me, cousin," he said, smiling again. Louisa-Margaretta wondered how she had not seen the sickness in that smile before now. He played at being the gay gentleman, all the while thinking only of money. She wondered how she had missed the many times that he had referred to people only as instruments provided for his own use. The peasants of the continental mountainsides where he liked to spend his days were "quaint, and terribly good at cooking, if you like large quantities," while the friends that he stayed with were "amusing, dear, and beautiful, at least enough to keep me tolerably amused for a month."

"You will turn yourself in," she said again, her voice faltering this time.

He raised his eyebrows. "And if I do not? You shall never be able to prove anything against me."

Louisa-Margaretta nearly told him that she had seen him poison her aunt, a lie he would not have been able to disprove, but she knew that he would not stop at killing her. The thought chilled her, and she took a step back.

He smiled, and she looked about for a weapon. There were so many pews, beautifully maintained thanks to Mrs Haddington, but they held nothing that would help her.

"I don't think I need to kill you," he said quietly, as if he had read her thoughts. "But I could if I wished to. I think you are going to help me find the records that I need. I have been in this horrid vestry, and I must say, I could not find a thing before. Your Mr St Clair and his predecessor have left things in a terrible muddle."

"I don't know where any of the records are," said Louisa-Margaretta, her mouth dry. "I have done nothing but have tea here, tea with Judith."

Her stomach turned when she thought of her friend. Even now, they were a stone's throw from the rectory, where Judith's sister, brothers, father, and aunt were likely preparing their own yule log and decorations. They would all be at home, and at any moment, one of them might come into the rectory to make certain that everything was prepared for the services they would hold that evening, as well as the one on Christmas Day.

It was as if Theo had read her thoughts, and she saw the

sick grin again. "Yes, your little friend would be very helpful. I'll go and ask her father for the records, shall I? I'm sure that if I flash my dagger, he will be most helpful."

Louisa-Margaretta started. "I'll find it! Let me into the vestry. Whatever it is, I can find it."

"Excellent. Once we have burned it, my dear cousin, you may leave. And if you value your life or that of your friend, I should say no more about all this. Our aunt and uncle were suicides. Unfortunate, I should say, but theirs is not the worst circle of hell."

"You won't find it," said a voice from the shadows, and the door of the vestry opened all the way.

Both Louisa-Margaretta and Theo whirled around to see Judith standing there, a candle in her hand. Her face looked pale but calm in its light.

"The book you are looking for is with the Haddingtons," she said. "I took the liberty of bringing it over with me today, and you won't be able to retrieve it."

"Judith," said Louisa-Margaretta, her voice already risen half an octave in fear. "Judith, he has a knife!"

Her friend, however, only advanced closer, holding the candle. "You wish to inherit," she said. "If you are indeed Mr Horace Ramsbury's first son, his fortune will now be yours."

Theo snorted. "His fortune is mine," he said. "And I will spend it as I wish, far from here. I already have all the records from my birth and his marriage. My mother and father's marriage was not some sad little affair, hushed up by the family. In this family, sorry little weddings seem to be rather a tradition. They wished me to marry my little cousin Louisa-Margaretta so she would not be tainted with scandal! Goodness, what a joke that would have been."

Judith's eyes flitted over to Louisa-Margaretta, who shook her head. Let Theo insult her, only let him leave. She prayed her friend would tell some lie to placate the madman, but

Judith came closer, the candle in her hand barely flickering in the afternoon light.

"Your father's first marriage, as you know," she said, "was to a fallen woman whom he met in London. He was very nearly disowned, but the great irony is that the marriage was perfectly legitimate and resulted in his first son."

"A bastard," snapped Theo. "There is no way of knowing whether he is my father's. But I can say he is almost certainly not. My father was taken in by a whore."

"The son," said Judith, as if she had not heard him, "was taken in by a childless couple in the family, your aunt and uncle. It was thought to be best after the boy's mother died suddenly and your father, in his grief, found that he could not care for the child. This childless couple were relatives of modest means. Their fortune went to him after both of them died, but it was hardly enough to support him. He was forced to choose between caring for his two young daughters and continuing his work as a physician. With such a fortune as your father's, he would not be forced to choose."

"Nobody can inherit two fortunes in this way," snarled Theo.

"In fact, many people can," said Judith. "The primary claim, of course, is that of a firstborn son on his father's estate. And that certainly applies here. All that is needed to prove it is the record of the marriage and that of the birth. The Haddingtons, who had the record of the marriage in Gretna Green, are now in possession of both."

Theo was still flushed with anger, and Louisa-Margaretta feared he might kill them both to keep the truth quiet somehow. She had believed Judith when her friend told her in the music room that Theo was guilty, but seeing his motives exposed made him seem more terrible in her eyes.

"So you only wished for the money," said Louisa-Margaretta, trying to keep her voice calm. "And if my uncle had given it to you? Did you give him a chance to destroy the record, or would you have killed him either way?"

"You forget our dear, dear aunt," sneered Theo. "She was always going on about coming up in Gretna Green, dropping hints of the marriages she had seen there, including that of my father with Ephraim's filthy mother. Besides, Ephraim endeared himself to my father somehow, though old Horace never worked up the nerve to tell that idiot he was going to inherit a fortune."

He was breathing heavily now. "The records would not have mattered if either of them had lived. They were both determined to give away what has always been mine."

He made for the door, and Louisa-Margaretta looked at Judith. She wished she could keep him from escaping, but she would need to let Godiva rest as long as she could if she were to have a chance. "You wished to go to Gretna Green yourself," she said, "and make an imprudent marriage. But Uncle Horace prevented it. That must have rankled when you found out what he'd done."

At this, her cousin turned slowly, and she immediately regretted her words. Though she had been trying to delay him, she was terrified.

"He was an old hypocrite," he said. "Always trying to get me to come back and return to Oxford or at least take up a position befitting a gentleman in the army. And all the while, he had his own secrets."

"How did you find out?" said Judith. "It must have been quite a shock."

He shook his head. "Some old biddy near here, a Mrs Maxwell. I have been meaning to leave her family a bit of cake, too, as a farewell present. I am sure if I reach their little cottage quickly enough, they will have eaten it all before any ladies can come to call. I must hope that they will give Mrs Maxwell the largest piece."

His smile was chilling, and he started for the door.

For the first time, Louisa-Margaretta could see genuine panic in her friend's face.

"Stop!" said Judith, running after him, and there was the flash of a dagger.

Louisa-Margaretta was with her friend in an instant. It was worse than she had imagined. Theo was gone, but she could not think of him, not when he had plunged his dagger into Judith's head. Louisa-Margaretta turned to stone, Judith in her arms, her tears flowing as she gasped for air. She dared not touch the dagger handle. She was afraid to touch Judith's head, but she saw how the knife had cut some hair away.

Judith's eyes were not open, and Louisa-Margaretta took her hand.

"Judith!" she cried. "Judith, it is all right. It is all right. Please, I am with you."

Those were the last words she managed to say before her mother pulled her away. As if in a dream, she saw her cousin Morgan racing into the room, yelling for his brother, and she heard a commotion from the next room, the one that Judith had entered holding her candle.

When the door opened, she saw that her cousin Theo was held fast by Mr Haddington and Mr St Clair, whose thin frame seemed to have concealed some measure of strength, but she was beyond caring.

She could not take her eyes from Judith.

❧ 48 ❧

"Happy Christmas, dears," said Mrs Haddington to Miriam St Clair and her aunt as they took off their coats, handing them to servants. Judith followed with her father and three brothers, wincing a bit at their loud voices. Moses and Joseph were always nearly yelling, and only Aaron showed any ability to speak in quiet tones, though he often forgot. When they were all through the door, she marveled at the decorations. The snow outside was glistening, and cold air came into the hall until the door was shut.

"I've always found mistletoe to be a most unseemly tradition," their hostess continued, walking closely with Miss Leah St Clair without noticing that the lady clearly wished to withdraw her arm. "So I have made a praying ball." She gestured to the decoration. "See, it is just as beautiful as what they call a 'kissing ball,' but one prays under it! You all must join me."

"We have said many prayers today in church," said Miriam, puzzled. "Is this the fashion, then, in London?"

"Fashions may come and go, my dear, but your spiritual nourishment is not something that can ever be neglected!"

insisted Mrs Haddington, surrendering Miss Leah St Clair's arm and holding Miss Miriam St Clair's instead.

"That is Mama's way of saying that, no, it is not in fashion anywhere," said a voice they all recognised, and Louisa-Margaretta joined them with a smile. "This is something that only exists at Wycliff Castle."

Aunt Leah took her nephews in hand, shepherding them over to the staircase to look at a particularly beautiful display. Louisa-Margaretta took Judith's arm, drawing her towards the parlour.

"You must sit down," she said. "You look pale."

"I've never known you to be such an old woman," teased Judith. "I am quite well, only I know my hair is looking very ill indeed. As you can see, I have very little to call my own, so after your cousin ruined the beautiful wig that Aunt Leah bought in town, I was left with almost nothing."

"I'm sure that I have something," said Louisa-Margaretta, looking rather uncertain.

Judith laughed at this. "The only person in this household with hair that matches mine is your father," she said. "And I'm afraid he hasn't kept any sorts of ornaments about in case of clumsy knife attacks. Truly, after I came to, I was well."

Still, Louisa-Margaretta forced her friend to sit down in the parlour. The boar's head would not be served for some time yet. First, there would be an interlude for the guests to admire the decorations.

"I worry much more about you," said Judith frankly. "In your condition, all that riding in the snow, and then the shock of the attack? Has a doctor seen you?"

Louisa-Margaretta frowned. "My condition?"

Judith looked about then lowered her voice. They were still alone in the parlour.

"The . . . you know. Well. The baby," she said, her voice hushed.

Louisa-Margaretta's reply was not hushed in the slightest. "Baby! What baby?"

Judith blinked. "The reason you are here in Derbyshire, and your parents wished you to marry? Are you not in a certain condition?"

Louisa-Margaretta started laughing then grew more serious as she described the trouble that had driven her from London. "A gentleman asked for my hand," she said. "My parents did not approve in the slightest. But there was nothing like that in it, Judith! Goodness, a baby? Perhaps if there had been one, they would have married me off right away, in spite of all their objections."

"They may yet reconsider," said Judith, thoughtfully. "Clearly, their matchmaking has amounted to nothing."

Louisa-Margaretta raised her eyebrows. "I would not say nothing."

"Oh?" Judith said. "Is there a gentleman asking for your hand?"

"There may be, soon. I admire my cousin Ephraim," said Louisa-Margaretta. "And ever since you scolded him, he has become a bit more amiable in his behaviour. But I am not sure that is quite enough when speaking of a marriage. After all, my cousin is in need of a wife who can help him cope with a whole Pandora's box of family secrets. He had never known that Uncle Horace was his father, and now, he has a vast fortune and an estate of his own. His daughters could do with a stepmother, as well, but I am not sure I would be up to the task."

"Then what will you do?" asked Judith. "As I am a spinster with no romantic prospects at all, I'm afraid I insist on knowing."

Louisa-Margaretta's face softened. "I have been so occupied with you, I have not thought of a way to get word to my intended," she said. "Or, not my intended, truly. I know nothing of him, and I know that no letter of mine will be able to leave the village. But if I write to him, is there any chance that you might . . ."

"Of course!" said Judith. "You may even have a moment to write a letter now, before we have to go and feign rapture over the boar's head."

"But I love the boar's head! You're telling me that you . . . ?"

"Despise it, yes. It is a brutal, heathen custom, and terrible for one's digestion. But I will make my 'oohs' and 'aahs' creditable for your mother's sake."

Louisa-Margaretta smiled at her friend, and Judith could see the hope in her expression. "I will write, then," she said. "But I need more than one moment stolen from a party. When I have the letter ready, I will tell you, and our subterfuge shall begin then."

They joined the party that was still near the entrance admiring the decorations. Judith noticed that not all of the paintings were hideous. There was one portrait she rather liked. It must have belonged to the old family, but there was a sort of impishness in the eye of the subject that the painter must have deliberately set down.

She wandered about, admiring many of the things she saw, until she was stopped by Mr Morgan Ramsbury.

"I'm afraid we are now underneath Mrs Haddington's creation," he said, and Judith started. He was looking very handsome indeed, dressed for the day in full mourning. His clothing looked fine and very expensive. But she never had suspected him of being a dandy. Rather, as a handsome young man, he simply looked well in everything. Very well indeed.

"I'm sorry, Mr Ramsbury?"

Seeing her discomfort, he blushed as well. "It's not a kissing ball! Not that, if it were . . . well. My aunt, as you can imagine, has come up with a tradition all her own. This is called a praying ball."

Judith blinked. "A praying ball?" She wanted to say that she had already heard Mrs Haddington explain the concept, but all of her words seemed to have deserted her.

"Yes. So, those who are under it are meant to offer prayers. She thinks it far more wholesome than the decor that might be offered, say, in town or in some of the less pious country houses."

Judith looked over at Louisa-Margaretta. Her friend's knowing smile made her feel even more ill at ease, and suddenly, she recalled all the times that her friend had started speaking with Mr Morgan Ramsbury then gone silent as soon as she was within Judith's sight. Those conversations took on a new meaning now that she knew Louisa-Margaretta had no interest in her cousin, although now at least she did not think him a murderer. She had been trying to create opportunities for Judith to know the man better. Louisa-Margaretta had sensed, well before Judith could, that Mr Morgan Ramsbury had begun to capture her regard.

"Well, Mr Ramsbury," she said, trying not to blush. "I pray that you have a happy Christmas in spite of your grief and that we have a chance to play a tune or two together at last."

"Miss St Clair," he said, "I wish you the same and would be most honoured if you would join me."

Agnes hurried over then, without noticing the praying ball above, and breathed, "Is it not wonderful? A stranger has arrived and is to have Christmas dinner with all of us! Only she is quite certain that she met a ghost on the path."

"She could not have met a ghost, Agnes," said Mr Morgan Ramsbury, and Judith could not decide whether she was pleased or dismayed that their conversation had been interrupted.

"Why does she think she saw a ghost?" said Judith, curious in spite of herself.

"I don't think I saw a ghost," they heard an old woman saying. "I did see one."

Judith and Mr Morgan Ramsbury exchanged a glance, and Judith saw both trust and amusement in his eyes. It was an expression that was to sustain her for days to come.

As one, they moved toward their visitor and the various Haddingtons and St Clairs who were gathered about her, chattering and smiling.

"A ghost!" said Louisa-Margaretta, her clear voice rising above all of them. "That sounds like good fun."

ABOUT THE AUTHOR

Eve Tarrington is a Jane Austen fanatic. She has written dozens of books, but this is her first historical mystery set in the Regency era. She is thankful to her readers, her family, and her friends.

Would you like to know when Eve Tarrington is putting out a new novel? You're in luck! Join the mailing list at tena ciousteacuppress.com/eveTnews. You'll get an email when a new book is coming out.